Youn Hee
& Me

C. S. ADLER

Youn Hee
& Me

Harcourt Brace & Company

San Diego   New York   London

Library of Congress Cataloging-in-Publication Data
Adler, C. S. (Carole S.)
Youn Hee & me/C. S. Adler.—1st ed.
p.   cm.
Summary: Caitlin finds out that bringing her adopted Korean brother's eleven-year-old sister into their home requires patience and understanding, but gradually they become a real family.
ISBN 0-15-200073-9   ISBN 0-15-200376-2 (pbk.)
[1. Adoption—Fiction. 2. Brothers and sisters—Fiction.
3. Family—Fiction. 4. Korean Americans—Fiction.]   I. Title.
PZ7.A26145Yo 1995
[Fic]—dc20   94-31060

The text was set in Fairfield Medium.

Designed by Kaelin Chappell

First edition

A B C D E

Printed in Hong Kong

To Maya Simone Adler—
welcome to the world and a wonderful life.

Thanks to my friend Haeja Hwang,
who kindly checked this manuscript for
language appropriateness and who taught
me the game of *yout*

Thanks also to Mam Soon Lee,
who patiently answered my questions on
Korean culture, particularly with
regard to children

Chapter One

My little brother Simon and I were kicking
a soccer ball around by the light of the street
lamps that had come on early that dark November evening. Mom whizzed into our
driveway and opened the car door to yell that
she wanted to see us in the kitchen, pronto.
Just then Simon took a head ball that would
have cracked any other five-year-old's
skull.

"Be there in a second, Mom," I called as
I leaped to knock the ball away from the
azalea bushes and our bay window. Probably
my normally cool, calm mother was agitated
because the school had called her about
something either Simon or I had done. That
day I'd gotten lunchroom detention just for
snatching a few baseball caps. But Simon,
being Simon, might have done worse. It
didn't mean a thing that he'd answered

1

"Fine" when I'd asked him how school had gone. He always says "Fine," no matter what.

"Leave that ball, Caitlin, and come in here," Mom said. Her voice had the knife edge that makes even Simon hop to. We were at her heels as she turned on the kitchen lights.

She aimed her blue spotlights on us and said, "You won't believe this, of course. I didn't either at first, but it's certainly exciting news." She smiled at Simon, who was frowning at her.

"Spit it out, Mom," I urged.

She took a deep breath and let it out. "Well, it seems that Simon has a sister in an orphanage in Korea."

"WHAT?" I asked. "How come we never heard about her before?" We'd adopted Simon when he was two from church people who told us he was an orphan without any brothers or sisters. "How old is she?" I asked Mom before she could answer my first question.

"Just your age, Caitlin. She's eleven."

"Simon," I said. "How come you never told us you had a sister?"

2

"You're my sister," he said. His black eyes curled up above his chipmunk cheeks in an irresistible smile.

"Right, but now you have another one, a Korean one," I said. "Don't you remember her?"

He shrugged.

"He probably *doesn't* remember, Caitlin." Mom was still standing there in her dress-up-for-work heels. She hadn't even heaved her two-ton purse off her shoulder yet.

"You're sure this is really his sister?" I asked.

"No question. I got an official letter from the head of the orphanage where Youn Hee—that's her name—has been for three years. It seems they only found out by accident that her brother is alive. Everyone assumed Simon had been killed in the train wreck along with their parents."

"So are we going to adopt her, too?" I asked. Because if Simon had a sister, she was automatically part of our family, wasn't she?

"I don't know." Mom ran her fingers through her already messy thatch of hair and dislodged a pen she'd probably forgotten was tucked in there. I picked up the pen and eased her purse off her shoulder.

"Thanks, Caitlin," she said absently. "I've been thinking about what to do ever since I first heard, and I'm still not sure. That's why I want your input. This affects us all."

"But, Mom," I said slowly, "the holidays are coming. How can we eat our turkey or open our presents while Simon's sister is stuck in an orphanage in Korea? We don't have any choice. We *have* to adopt her."

Mom rumpled my hair. "I know you're a generous kid, sweetie, but let's not decide too quickly. We wouldn't be inviting this child for a visit. We'd be offering to share the rest of our lives with her."

I chewed on my lip awhile, thinking about having a sister my own age. If she shared my room, we could talk things over at night in our beds. She'd understand that even when I did try hard to study for tests, I couldn't get the good grades that would please Mom. I could throw a ball better than most kids, but I couldn't ace a test. Having a sister who understood how bad that made me feel would be a comfort.

"Do I got a brother, too?" Simon asked Mom—a little too hopefully to suit me.

"What do you mean, do you have a brother?" I growled at him. "You have me, don't you?"

"Yeah, but a brother is more better," he said.

I put my hands on my hips and bent down to stick my long nose against his pudgy one. "What do you mean, a brother would be better? Don't I play soccer with you? Don't I clean up the mess when you fill the bathroom full of soap bubbles? Don't I give you the pickles off my hamburgers?"

Simon grinned amiably and rubbed noses Eskimo-style with me. I grabbed him and hugged hard while he tried to squirm free.

"OK, you two, sit down at the kitchen table and pay attention now," Mom said. Simon and I sat.

"This house is pretty small," Mom began. "Squeezing another person into it would be tough."

"I hope she's neat," I said, thinking of the disaster area that was Simon's bedroom.

"And what if we agree to adopt her and you don't like her?" Mom asked.

"Then Caitlin and me won't play with her," Simon said.

Mom groaned. Well, what did she expect from a five-year-old? "Don't worry, Mom, I like everybody," I said to reassure her. Immediately two kids on my basketball team I didn't like all that much popped into my mind. One's so sneaky she can get away with fouling on the basketball court, and the other one whines whenever the coach makes her return the ball to the locker. Come to think of it, I'm not wild about my uptight father either, but that doesn't matter because I don't see him much.

"It will mean sacrifices on all our parts," Mom warned.

"What about college?" I asked. Sometimes I try to think like an adult so Mom isn't the only one in the family. "You can't afford to send us all, can you? . . . Of course, I'll probably get a basketball scholarship." I crossed my fingers for luck. "And Simon'll get some kind of athletic scholarship, too, so it won't be too bad, Mom."

I don't know why that struck Mom as funny, but she began to laugh.

"Forget it," she said. She waved her

hands in dismissal or defeat or whatever. "Family council's ended. I'll make dinner and we'll talk about this again later."

"Can I go watch my program?" Simon asked.

"Sure," Mom said. And Simon bounced off to the TV in the living room.

"So much for his interest in another sister," I said.

"He probably just can't take it in. *I* can't take it in," Mom said. "I haven't been able to concentrate at work since the letter came."

"Can I see the letter, Mom?"

"If you want, but the English is kind of hard to read. Basically, it says that a woman who came to work at the orphanage knew the poor farm family that found Simon after the train wreck. It seems the family didn't know anything about him. They just took him home and took care of him unofficially until they couldn't afford to feed him anymore. Then they brought him to the church."

"It's no wonder they couldn't feed him," I said. "Simon's appetite belongs in the *Guinness Book of World Records*. You know

7

what he had for a snack when we came home from school, Mom?"

"Caitlin, do you want to discuss this or not?" Mom asked. She was crouched in front of the vegetable bin at the refrigerator. She'd gotten wide as a comfortable armchair once she'd relaxed and stopped dieting after Dad left us.

I took out the vegetable bin and set it on the counter for her.

She said, "You do remember what a hard time you had getting used to Simon, don't you?"

Did I ever! I'd been an only child for eight years, and becoming a big sister to a Korean-speaking two-year-old had been tough. I didn't even *like* Simon the first year. In fact, I hated him—sometimes a lot. It wasn't just that I had to learn to share; it was that Simon kicked and hit me and broke my Disney character collection and wouldn't do what I told him. Mom called him her little samurai. That's a Japanese warrior. I don't know if they have them in Korea, but Simon sure was at war here, especially at war with me. It took him more than a year to settle down and become fun to live with. Of course

8

now, if anyone asked me, I'd say I have a terrific little brother.

"Youn Hee's a girl," I said. "And she's eleven, not two. It'll be fine, Mom."

All of a sudden Mom hugged me. "Oh, Caitlin," she said, "I don't know why I'm pretending we have a choice. Now that we know she exists, we do have to adopt her, don't we?"

"Right." I smiled, glad to see Mom back to acting normal. My mother's all heart. She'd do anything for a kid who needs help. I'm sure that's why they promoted her to director of the Child Care and Development Agency. Her whole career's been in social work dealing with kids. And she seemed pretty happy living with Simon and me with no other adult to help her. Another kid in the family wouldn't faze her. Nothing fazed Simon. As for me, I kind of liked the idea.

When I kissed Mom good night later, she asked, "Do you understand what an impact adopting Youn Hee will have on you, Caitlin? I mean, especially on you. I'm gone all day. You're the one who'll have to integrate her into our lives and keep her happy. It may become a burden. What if it keeps you from your sports activities, or if she's not a girl you can relate to?"

"Mom, relax," I said confidently. "I'm going to love having a sister." And I wouldn't listen to another word.

In bed that night, I ran through girls' names to figure out what Youn Hee's American name could be. We got Simon from Si Won, mispronounced a little. Youn Hee didn't sound like anything that I could think of. Well, she might like picking her own name when she got here. I wondered if she'd be active and outgoing like Simon. I hoped she'd like me. She had better if we were going to be sisters.

Chapter Two

I couldn't wait to get to school the next morning to tell my friends about our family expansion plan. I rolled Simon—who wakes up in slow motion—out of his bed and aimed him at the bathroom. Then I joined Mom for breakfast. She was drinking coffee from the giant "Best Mom" mug I'd given her for Mother's Day, while she read stuff from her briefcase.

"Do you think Youn Hee'll get here by Christmas?" I asked her.

Mom tucked the papers back in the briefcase. "These things take time, Caitlin. It might be months or even years. You'll have to be patient."

"Oh, boy," I said. "Just what Simon and I are best at—Not. Can you try and get a picture of her at least, Mom?" On the refrigerator door, we still had the one we got of Simon before he came.

"I'll try." Mom turned toward Simon's picture with a misty-eyed smile. "It's hard to believe what a little twig of a kid he was. Nobody who knew him then would recognize him now."

We stared at each other, snagged on the same thought. What if Youn Hee didn't recognize Simon?

"We have lots to decide before she gets here, Caitlin," Mom said briskly. "Like, where are we going to put her?"

"In my room with me," I said. "Where else?"

"I was hoping you'd say that. It would be a nasty trick to put anyone in that garbage dump for toys Simon lives in. She'll be overwhelmed enough as it is by everything here."

"Why? Simon wasn't."

"Simon takes the world as he finds it," Mom said. "Youn Hee could be another story."

"She's going to be terrific," I said with conviction.

It was cold out that morning. Car exhausts made skinny clouds long as kite tails, and

12

frost iced the lawns. Simon and I joined Marie at the bus stop. Her nose was red and drippy from the cold. Marie's an eighth-grader and I like her OK, even though I can't understand why she won't try out for the basketball team when she's so tall. She says she hates sports. How can anybody hate sports?

"Marie," Simon asked, "are you going to marry a giraffe?"

Marie flinched. "Who told you to ask me that, Simon?"

"Nobody. A boy said it in school, that you'll have to marry—"

"She's not *that* tall, Simon," I leaped to Marie's defense. "She just looks tall to you because you're so short."

"I'm not short!" Simon protested. Immediately the corners of his lips cut downward. Now *his* feelings were hurt. Some days you can't win.

"You think you're tall then?" I asked.

"I think you stink," he said, and tried to kick me, but I grabbed him and wrestled him to the ground.

"You're getting your new jacket dirty, Caitlin," Marie said.

"Help me hold him," I said. "He's strong as an ox."

"Tiger," Simon said. "Strong as a tiger."

"Yeah, well, just don't try and kick me again, or you'll be dead tiger meat." I let him go and examined my new, mostly white, down-filled jacket. It only had a few smudges.

Just because I had to tell somebody, I gave Marie the news about Youn Hee.

"Simon has a sister?" she asked. "How come he never said anything about her?"

"Well, he couldn't talk English when he came."

"He probably doesn't even remember her," Marie said. "Do you remember *anything* about Korea, Simon?"

"I came on the plane," Simon said.

"Right," I said. "You remember that, don't you?"

He shook his head. "Mommy told me."

"And before you got on the plane—do you remember your family?"

He glared at me and wouldn't answer.

"What do you want from the kid? He doesn't even know he's Korean," Marie said.

"I'm not Korean. I'm American. See?" Simon saluted smartly.

"You teach him that, Caitlin?" Marie asked.

"No. He could have picked it up from TV."

Simon's friend Andy came trudging toward the bus stop. His glasses were falling off the end of his nose as usual, and he had so much outer clothing on, he could barely walk. His folks had just moved here from the South, so they probably were nervous about upstate New York winters.

"Andy!" Simon yelled joyfully. He galloped to meet Andy and nearly knocked him over with a friendly whack on the back.

"Two Koreans in the family," Marie said to me. "You'll be outnumbered, Caitlin."

"What do you mean outnumbered? And anyway, Simon's American. He said so himself."

"Yeah, but he looks Korean. He's got those slit eyes and that tan skin."

"Slit eyes? Simon's the cutest kid in his class. What are you, prejudiced or something?"

"No. I'm just saying, you can pretend all you want, but Simon doesn't look like your brother. He's got slant eyes and black hair, and you've got curly hair and blue eyes."

15

So I hit her. Not for *what* she was saying but for *how* she said it. She made it sound bad that Simon looked Korean. Simon may not look like me, but we're both high-energy kids and everybody likes us—except maybe a few teachers and some aides and the principal. He's my brother all right. No question.

"I'm not speaking to you anymore, Caitlin," Marie cried. She was holding her arm where I'd socked her. Marie's being two years older than me and six inches taller doesn't matter because she is a wimp.

"I'm sorry I hit you," I said. "But what you said made me mad."

"What did I say?" She looked bewildered.

"Here comes the bus," Simon yelled. He dragged Andy into line in front of us and set his own toes at the edge of the curb to be first on.

"You said— Oh, never mind, Marie. Just take it back."

She rubbed her arm some more and said, "OK, I take it back, whatever it was. But I don't want anything more to do with you, Caitlin."

That was OK with me. I didn't want anything much to do with her. My real

16

friends—Audrey and Bud and Denise—
think Simon is the greatest, which he is,
and the shape of his eyes has nothing to do
with that.

The bus driver held up our bus so he could
yell at us about making so much noise that
he couldn't drive safely. And he looked right
at Simon and me even though we'd been
quiet the whole trip. Anyway, that made us
late for homeroom, so I had to wait until
lunchtime to talk to my friends.

The minute Audrey set her tray down
across from me, I told her about how I was
going to get a sister from Korea. "Really?"
she said. "Listen, Caitlin, if you want some
extra brothers and sisters, you can have
mine."

"You don't mean that, Audrey."

"Sure she does." It was Bud speaking.
He'd just plunked his lunch tray down next
to my soup and crackers. "Audrey'd like
being an only child so her folks could spend
all their money on her."

"I'm not greedy," Audrey said. "I just
want to go skiing this winter on new skis
instead of hand-me-downs."

Bud gave her a pity party *"Awww!"* and

17

Audrey blew her straw wrapper at him. Denise sat down next to Audrey. Of my three friends, Denise is the most perfect. That girl's good at everything, not just sports and schoolwork; she even plays trumpet in the band and she's class secretary. She doesn't say much though. Actually, Audrey's more fun. Like me, she's a sports nut and a C student, except she's good in math. Bud is as smart as Denise, but more easygoing, and he's so softhearted, anybody's trouble makes him ooze sympathy.

I told Bud and Denise my news, but when they pressed me for details, I had to admit I didn't have any yet. "I'll keep you posted," I told them.

"That's really exciting, Caitlin," Bud said. "I hope she gets here fast."

What Denise said was that getting a sister your own age sounded better than having a baby born into the family because it was less work and more fun. I hadn't thought of it that way.

Audrey didn't say much that lunch period. When we were in the girls' room after lunch, I asked, "So how's that yoga class? Is it making you taller?" Her aunt had told her yoga would stretch her at least two inches.

"Not yet," she said.

"You're not still mad at me because I couldn't take it with you, are you, Audrey?"

"I'm not mad," she said. "But Caitlin, you couldn't take the yoga class because you have to watch Simon after school, and now his sister's coming. You're never going to have time to do anything with me."

"Oh, come on, Audrey!" I thought fast and offered, "Maybe Youn Hee'll help baby-sit so I can do things with you again."

"I sure hope so," Audrey said. But I could see she doubted it.

The photograph that Mom finally brought home gave me a funny feeling. Youn Hee was so pretty! She had long, straight hair and a cute kitten face. We couldn't have looked more different. I've got curly brown hair and a kind of horse face with elastic lips and bulgy blue eyes. I'm not really as ugly as that sounds, but I'm not pretty either, and I certainly don't look delicate. Youn Hee was as delicate as one of those look-don't-touch costume dolls. We put the photo on the refrigerator next to Simon's, but it didn't feel right until the morning I came down and Mom had added a school photo of me. I liked that, having the three of us there with Simon in the middle.

Thanksgiving was OK. Dad hadn't asked Simon and me to spend the holiday with him again, and as usual Mom worked hard to convince us it wasn't that he didn't love us or anything like that. Actually, I didn't care, and neither did Simon. I mean, I'd have liked it if Dad had at least asked, but behaving perfectly enough to suit him and his new wife wears me out. Anyway, Mom and Simon and I went out for a turkey dinner, just the three of us.

A couple of days later Simon, his buddy Andy, and I were playing soccer with a seven-year-old future hood, and the kid stepped on Andy's glasses. So I accidentally on purpose knocked him over. I was sitting on the little bully, who was yelling, "Get off me, you big butt-face," when Mom pulled the car into the driveway.

"Caitlin, Simon," she called, too excited to notice what was going on. "Say good-bye to your friends and come in the house. Emergency session."

I untangled myself and hauled Simon indoors. "Why can't we play?" he complained. "It's not dark yet."

"Because," Mom said dramatically, "your sister's coming tomorrow, and we have to get the house ready for her."

"Youn Hee is coming tomorrow? It's not even Christmas," I said.

"Some other kid got sick, and they sent Youn Hee in her place so as not to waste the plane ticket. Caitlin, you better make space in your closet. And Simon, you go pick up your toys so she doesn't see what a messy kid you are."

"I'm not a messy kid," Simon protested. His lips went down and he went into his stubborn warrior stance.

"That's not fair, Mom," I said. "Simon picked up his room. I helped him."

"You mean last weekend? Have you looked in there since?"

It was true Simon had a building project going. He had used his boxes full of blocks and Legos and farm sets and trucks and cars and plastic figures to make a toy town that went up and down over his bed and chair and table on empty cartons that he said were mountains and along boards that he said were streets. He'd dragged me in to admire it last night while I was catching up with overdue homework, the get-it-in-or-you'll-get-a-D kind. He had also kicked off his underpants so they were hanging from the curtain rod, and he'd dotted the furniture and floor with dirty socks.

"I'll help you pick up again, Simon," I said.

Mom hustled us both off saying, "And Caitlin, make space in your dresser, too. Tonight we'll go to the mall. She's got to have a bed and all kinds of stuff. I'll make a list."

"Why not wait until she gets here so she can pick out what she wants?" I asked.

"We're supposed to have presents to make her feel welcome. She'll expect them, I'm told. Mush, move it. We'll eat a frozen pizza tonight."

"Yippee!" Simon said.

Straightening his room took a while, and then I still had to empty two dresser drawers and half my closet. I'm not much of a collector, which is why it's easy for me to keep my room neat. When I get tired of something, I just give it to somebody who can use it. That way I even feel good about getting rid of stuff. I left the games and my shelf of mystery books alone, figuring Youn Hee and I could share them, and stuck my summer clothes in boxes in the basement. I even labeled them.

"So I'm ready for her," I told Mom. "Except I want to buy her something from my allowance money. What do you think she'd like?"

Mom was dishing up the pizza. "A hairbrush?"

"A hairbrush!" I was indignant. "You get her that. How about a book, maybe a mystery?"

"Caitlin, she doesn't know English."

"A picture book then, or how about a dictionary?"

"I bought a Korean–English dictionary of sorts," Mom said. "Simon, you're supposed to eat the pizza, not wash your face with it. Where's your napkin?"

I was still trying to think of what special gift I could get for Youn Hee while Mom was explaining to the department store salesman why she needed immediate delivery on the twin bed and chair she'd just ordered.

"We only deliver to your area on Thursdays," he kept saying. The bed wouldn't come for a week. "Relax, Mom. She can share my bed," I said.

I wondered if maybe a bowl of goldfish would appeal to Youn Hee. But by the time Mom finished buying a pillow and bedding and identical flannel nightgowns, one in women's petite for me and one in a girl's size ten for Youn Hee, the pet shop was closed.

Simon had gotten his present for her. It was a big lollipop coiled like a colorful rag rug. He'd begged for that lollipop the last time we came to the mall, and my bet was he was hoping Youn Hee would share it with him.

"Now what am I going to get her?" I wailed.

"Caitlin, it's no big deal. Give her a hug and tell her you'll take her to buy something she wants later."

"But she can't speak English. How's she going to understand me?"

"Say it in Korean then. Look up the

24

words. The sheets are on the table at home."
Mom had gotten out the sheets of Korean
words and phrases that the adoption people
had given her to learn simple stuff from before we got Simon. Like *"Pyunso kalay?"*—
"Do you need to go to the bathroom?" And
"cha ka da"—"good boy." Since Simon didn't
remember any Korean, he was no help.

On the way home I saw him picking at
the cellophane wrapper of the lollipop.

"Don't, Simon," I said. "It's not a gift if
you lick it first."

He stuck out his lower lip, but he stopped
picking.

Simon slept that night. Maybe Mom did,
too. I was too excited to fall asleep until way
past midnight. Before the next midnight, I
was going to have not only a little brother
but a sister, and my life would be changed
forever.

Chapter Three

After the mad rush around the mall, I felt
like we were creeping toward Youn Hee's
five o'clock train arrival the next day. Time
stretched out like an unbreakable high-
tech rubber band. I was sure the clocks in
my classroom had stopped. Three teachers
yelled at me for not paying attention, and I
goofed up a math quiz on stuff Audrey had
drilled into my head last weekend. She was
really disgusted with me.

At lunch she said, "Only you would be
brainless enough to volunteer to share your
bedroom with a total stranger, Caitlin." See,
Audrey thought having your own bedroom
was luxury living because she didn't have a
chance of it with six kids in her family.

"I won't mind," I said.

"Oh yeah? Suppose she's a vampire?" Audrey's been hung up on horror books lately.

"Or she could snore," Bud said. "Snoring's more likely than vampires."

"I hope she's in our class," Denise said in that quiet voice that somehow gets our attention.

"Why?" Audrey asked. "Caitlin's gotta have someplace to get away from her for a few hours a day."

"Well, in that picture Caitlin showed us, Youn Hee looks small," Denise said, "and I'm tired of being the smallest kid in the class."

"Small, but power packed," Bud said. He had a crush on Denise that had started in fifth grade and hadn't stopped even though she ignored it. Like now she was pretending she hadn't heard him.

"Hey, you guys," I told them. "I'm already nervous about this and you're not helping."

They gave me a chorus of "sorry's" followed by heavy silence, until Bud finally started telling knock-knock jokes. His favorite grandfather had taught them to him, which is probably why they struck Bud as hysterically funny.

I got home from school at three and vacuumed my room so it would look nice for

Youn Hee. Mom usually gets a cleaning service in, but I was so hyper I needed to do something. I hoped Youn Hee wasn't going to mind that my walls were covered with basketball posters. What if all those life-size jocks in uniform staring down at her kept her from sleeping? What if she wanted pictures of kittens or Disney characters instead? But I loved my basketball posters, and some of them were signed!

"Caitlin," Simon called. "Look at what I built."

I walked into his room and groaned. He'd dumped out the building blocks, plastic figures, and trucks he'd put away yesterday and was rebuilding his village. Only this time he was using sheets and blankets to make hills over the chairs and boxes.

"Aren't you excited about meeting your long-lost sister?" I asked him.

"Is she going to bring me a present?"

"I don't think so, Simon. She lived in an orphanage. That means she's poor."

"Oh." Simon went back to his building.

Actually, his village looked pretty cool. Youn Hee might even like it. I picked up some blocks and began to help him.

Mom got home early and made *bool-go-ghi,*

which is a Korean beef, soy sauce, sesame oil, and garlic dish she made for Simon when he came. He was Si Won then and he liked the stuff fine, but as it turned out, he likes any kind of food fine.

"Uh-oh, we used up all the Korean rice," Mom said. "Think she'll mind if I use American-style rice?"

"Mom, relax. She'll like everything." I wasn't that sure, but Mom was acting even more nervous than I was.

We had to drag Simon away from his TV program when it was time to leave for the train station.

"I don't know," Mom murmured in the car. "Maybe I shouldn't have been so impulsive."

"You did the right thing," I assured her. "We couldn't leave somebody that's related to us in an orphanage."

"If I were home all day, taking on another child would be fine," Mom said, "but I'm not, and to leave her alone in the house when she's been used to constant supervision. . . ."

"Alone? Mom, I'm going to be there. And Simon."

"I know," Mom said as if that didn't

comfort her. "Anyway I've done it now." She pulled into the Amtrak lot and found a parking space. The train was due in half an hour.

I was as fizzy as newly opened seltzer. "I think this is the most exciting moment of my life," I said.

"What would I do without you, Caitlin?" Mom asked, and she hugged me. "You're right, this is an adventure." She let go of me and crossed her fingers for luck, even though she claims not to be superstitious. "I just hope we survive it."

Simon raced around the station waiting room, then started walking on top of whatever seats didn't have people sitting in them. Mom told him to stop that, so he spent two minutes with an old man who offered him some Life Savers. Next time I looked he was *crawling* over the seats.

"Sit, Simon," Mom said in a final-bell voice. Simon sat. We had twenty minutes to go.

Simon started wriggling and said he had to go to the bathroom. I led him to the ladies' room, but he pointed to the skirted silhouette on the door and protested that he was a boy. Before I could grab him, he'd pushed open the door with the male silhouette and disappeared.

"Mom," I called, "what do I do now?" Mom had a thing about child molesters lurking in public bathrooms.

"Give him two minutes and go after him," she said. A teenage girl with a huge backpack snickered. I glared at her and started counting. Luckily, Simon came out before I got to 120.

We still had fifteen minutes to wait. I told Simon a story, his favorite kind, about a monster who tries to eat a little boy, but the little boy tricks the monster into a cage and sells him to the circus and buys a lot of candy with the money and has his picture in the paper and is admired by everyone.

"And he grew up to be president," Simon said.

"Yeah, president of a candy factory."

"No, United States president." Simon puffed himself up and reared back on his heels. "Like me."

"You're going to be president?"

"Yeah."

"Wow," I said. "Can I have your autograph?"

"Sure." Simon wrote a pretend one on my hand.

"Don't encourage him," Mom said when Simon bounded off to check out the candy machine. "You have to be born in this country to be eligible to run for president."

"You do? But that's not fair," I said.

"Nevertheless, it's a law."

"So Americans don't really trust anybody from another country?"

"Come on, Caitlin, don't get worked up over it. What are the chances that Simon's going to be disappointed when he gets old enough to run and finds out he can't? One in a million?"

"That's not the point," I said. "It's just wrong for everybody."

"Grow up to change it then," Mom said. Slyly she added, "Of course, if you want to have anything to do with the law, you'll need to get decent grades in school so that you can get a college degree and—"

"Forget it, Mom. I told you, I'm going to be a pro basketball player."

Mom groaned, "Oh, Caitlin!" It was one of the things she and Dad agreed on, that school learning was important and sports weren't. I wondered if Youn Hee was going to be a good student.

With five minutes still to go, I suggested taking Simon up on the platform for some fresh air. I needed some, too.

"The train may not be on time," Mom warned. But she came with us.

The open-air platform was long, dark, and cold. It was lit mostly by lights from the buildings that poked their heads up from the streets below. Simon took off running, and I kept pace with him in case he dived onto the tracks. Mom was right. The train was late, five minutes and then ten. I got tired of running and locked Simon in my arms to keep him still.

"No fair," he said as he struggled. "You're bigger than me."

Mom had her scarf around her nose; her eyes were tearing from the cold. "I hope Youn Hee's dressed warmly enough," she said.

I saw a light way down the track moving our way. "Here it comes," I yelled. My heart skittered crazily. "Simon, look, look. Your sister is coming," I said. "See that train?

She'll be on it, Simon. Stand next to us so she'll know we're her family."

The train's silver snout pushed up to the platform, which had suddenly filled with people. I didn't see Youn Hee until a uniformed conductor broke through the crowd holding a little girl's hand. Mom hustled toward her, and Simon and I pushed after her.

"I'm Mrs. Lacey," Mom told the conductor. She waved some kind of identification at him. Meanwhile I stared openmouthed at this tiny girl who didn't look any older than Simon. Her eyes weren't narrow either. They were as round as mine, but tilted at the ends and shiny with fear.

"Youn Hee?" I asked uncertainly.

"Hey, she's little," Simon said. "Is she my sister?"

Youn Hee just stared at us. "Yes, she's your sister," I said, and in case we'd upset her by acting as if we didn't know who she was, I gave her a big toothy grin to reassure her.

"Here," Simon said. He presented Youn Hee with the lollipop, which had gotten cracked in his pocket but was still wrapped at least.

She took it, murmuring something I couldn't catch. It sounded like Korean. Then she reached out to Simon, but he ducked behind me in a sudden fit of shyness.

Meanwhile the conductor stepped back on his train, and Mom got down to the business of welcoming her newest daughter. "I'm your mother, Youn Hee," Mom said in very slow Korean before she pulled Youn Hee into the folds of her winter coat in a big hug.

I hugged Youn Hee next and kissed her cheek even though she stiffened when I hugged her. "I'm your new sister," I said in English. I knew she couldn't speak it, but I figured she might understand some anyway. I even tried to say it in Korean. *"Neh ga uhn nee ya."*

Youn Hee's bowknot mouth opened and she began to wail.

"Oh dear," Mom said. "It's all right, Youn Hee. We're your family, and you're safe now." She put her arm around Youn Hee again and tried to steer her toward the stairs to the station. Youn Hee looked around wildly, but where could she escape? She let Mom drag her off.

Simon patted Youn Hee's arm when we

35

got to the car. "Don't be scared, little girl," he said.

Somewhere or other she'd dropped the lollipop, but she still had hold of her bag. Before Simon could notice his gift had been lost, I went back and found the lollipop on the steps and tried to give it to her. She wouldn't take it, so I gave it to Simon and got in the backseat. Simon sat in front with Mom. Youn Hee was scrunched against the back door, as far away from me as she could get. I smiled at her again so she'd know I wasn't planning to eat her, but she still looked terrified. Her hair was shorter than it was in the picture. She was pretty, but not the sister I had imagined getting. First of all, she seemed to be closer to Simon's age than to mine, and second of all, she obviously wasn't eager to be part of our family. I wondered if anyone had even asked her if she wanted to come. Maybe they'd just thrown her on the plane without giving her a chance to say whether she wanted to leave or not. Maybe she was feeling like we'd kidnapped her. And until she learned enough English we couldn't explain. No sense in me trying to learn more Korean either. Youn Hee obviously hated the way I spoke the little I'd managed to learn.

Suddenly my arms and legs felt like I'd tied lead weights to them. I sat there too heavy to budge, asking myself the question Mom had asked before: What had we gotten ourselves into?

Chapter Four

Youn Hee wouldn't eat the *bool-go-ghi* Mom had prepared to make her feel at home. Simon had second helpings and kept saying, "Um, good" to encourage Youn Hee, but she didn't even taste it.

As for the rice, she picked up her spoon and toyed with it, but she didn't eat that either. Mom poured her a glass of milk and one of water and one of apple juice. Youn Hee seemed puzzled by the three glasses, so Mom used the Korean word list to name them. Even then, Youn Hee just sat there and wouldn't touch anything.

"Do you think she's sick?" I asked.

"The poor child's probably just exhausted," Mom said. "We'll put her to bed. I'm sure she'll feel like eating tomorrow."

My new sister seemed so leery of me that I guessed she'd be afraid to share my bed.

"I'll sleep on the floor and let her have the bed, Mom," I offered.

"She might feel more secure if you're next to her," Mom told me. She took Youn Hee off to the bathroom and brought her back in the child's size-ten nightgown. It was way too big for her. "I had to show her how the plumbing worked," Mom said. "Every-thing's so unfamiliar to her. It's no wonder she looks scared."

I nodded and went off to use the bathroom myself. When I got back to my bedroom, Mom had left to answer the phone and Youn Hee was sitting on the bed holding her suit-case on her lap. Her feet didn't touch the floor.

"*Cham cha ra,*" I said. It was supposed to be Korean for "go to sleep" according to the list Mom had. I said it with a smile and got into bed to show her. She promptly slipped off the bed and stood there hanging on to that suitcase as if she meant to go back to Korea with it then and there. I patted the pillow next to mine and squeezed way over so she had plenty of room—more than half the bed. But she didn't budge.

What could I do? Tell her she was my

sister? But when I'd used the Korean word for that, she'd burst into tears. *"Cham cha ra?"* I asked.

She looked tired enough to sleep standing up, but other than eyeing me suspiciously, she didn't move. I wanted to call for Mom to help, but yelling would have scared Youn Hee for sure and Mom was still on the phone. I tried putting myself in Youn Hee's place. Yeah, I'd be tired and anxious, but I think I'd figure out from all the smiling and hugging that we were friendly. I think I'd try and smile back and trust us. Youn Hee wasn't trusting anybody.

I yawned and put my head down on my pillow, hoping she'd get the idea. But there she stood, on guard against her American sister, the ogre. Maybe if I nodded off, she'd feel safe enough to go to sleep herself. I hadn't slept much the past two nights and I was really tired. I closed my eyes, curled around my pillow, and promptly sank into sandman land.

When I woke up the next morning, Youn Hee was asleep on the floor with a blanket over her and her pillow next to her head. I figured the hump under the blanket beside her was the suitcase and wondered what she had in it that was so precious.

It took me a minute to remember I didn't have to go to school. The plan was for Mom and Simon and me to stay home with Youn Hee for her first day with us. I crept out of bed and used the bathroom. It was a relief to find Mom alone in the kitchen drinking coffee.

"So," she said, "how's it going?"

"Not too good. I think Youn Hee hates me."

"Oh, Caitlin, don't be silly."

"Well, she'd rather sleep on the floor than get in bed with me."

"Yes, I know. When I checked on you two last night, I covered her. But Korean children are used to sleeping on the floor. It was probably the bed that seemed strange to her, not you, sweetie."

"Simon never had a hard time with the bed."

"Oh, sure he did. Don't you remember, he kept falling out?"

"No. I must have slept through that."

"So did he." Mom laughed. "Your father

was around then. He . . . he thought it was odd to find Simon asleep on the floor every night." Her face always got a pained look whenever my father's name came up. Mom and he hadn't had a fighting divorce. I mean they hadn't yelled at each other a lot, but he really hurt her feelings bad when he left her.

"Dad found everything kids do odd," I said. "He's no kid lover."

"Not really, no . . . Well, Simon hasn't gotten up yet either. What do you think we should do with them today?"

"I don't know. Take Youn Hee to the mall and get her clothes maybe. She can't have much to wear in that suitcase."

"She's so tiny, isn't she? For an eleven-year-old, I mean," Mom said.

"You really think she is eleven?"

"Oh yes. They sent me a copy of her birth certificate."

"Then the first thing we better do is make her eat something," I said. "She's got a lot of growing to do."

"I was thinking about having cereal for breakfast," Mom said. Usually her face seems sunny even when she's not smiling, but today she was clouded over.

"Mom, are you still worried that we made a mistake?" I asked.

"Of course not," Mom said. "It's obvious Youn Hee needs us even if she doesn't know it yet."

It was funny. Now that Mom was sure, I wasn't.

It was another rubber-band day that stretched out unbelievably. Audrey called me and wanted to know if she could come over before school and meet my new sister.

"She's sleeping," I said. "I haven't even met her much myself."

"Oh. Well, then, do you want to shoot some baskets after school?"

"I better hang out here with her."

"What for? She's going to be with you the rest of your life, isn't she?"

"I guess."

"You don't sound happy about it, Caitlin."

"Audrey, I told you, I don't know what she's like yet."

"Yeah. Well, then why don't you come to the school playground with Bud and me. My sister's driving and she'll pick you up, too."

"I can't."

"OK, OK. Call me back if you change

your mind. . . . You going to be in school tomorrow?"

"I don't know. This is a big event in my life, Audrey. People don't get sisters every day, you know."

"Sure they do. I got two at once last year, and you didn't see me staying home."

I had to laugh. Audrey claims to hate her twin sisters. She says they do nothing but scream and keep her mother too busy to drive Audrey to basketball games. The twins will have to become ballplayers before Audrey can like them.

"Have fun with Bud," I told her, and hung up.

Denise called next. "Is your sister there?" she asked. "Can you talk?"

"I don't have anything to say yet," I said. "All she's done so far is sleep. She hasn't even eaten anything yet."

"Well, how did she look when she came?"

"Pretty. And small. Smaller than you, Denise. And scared."

"*Umm,*" Denise said and paused to think. "Well, if there's anything I can do to help, call me, Caitlin."

"Thanks." I said, and meant it. The best thing about Denise is she can understand how you're feeling without your having to bang her over the head with it.

Youn Hee didn't wake up until near dinnertime, and then she went to the bathroom, drank a glass of water, and went back to sleep on her spot on the bedroom floor.

Simon had spent the day playing with his village and whining for me to play with him.

"Tomorrow Simon goes to school," Mom said when she caught him leaping off the back of the couch onto me and the fancy cushions it had taken her years to needlepoint. "But we can't send Youn Hee yet. I leave it up to you, Caitlin. Do you want to stay home with her, or shall I take another day off?"

I knew Mom hated taking personal leave days. First of all, she felt responsible for being in the office to make sure things ran right, and second of all, she wanted to save those days for emergencies, like when one of us was sick. Besides, who was the one who'd wanted a sister? I asked myself. Me, I had to answer myself honestly.

"I'll stay home," I said.

"Good girl. I knew I could count on you."

Mom sounded relieved. "But you'd better go slow with Youn Hee. Show her things and let her get used to the house. You can try her out on whatever you think she might like to eat. Maybe heat up some beef broth? You can go next door to Hettie if you need anything. Or call me, and I'll come home right away."

When I turned eleven, I told Mom I could take responsibility for Simon after school, and Mom arranged with Hettie Rosenberg that she would baby-sit only if I asked her. Hettie used to watch Simon every day after nursery school, but she had her own grandchildren to keep her busy now, so she was glad to leave him to me. I liked being in charge. Besides, Mom's office was just a fifteen-minute drive from our house across the river in Schenectady, so she could get home fast enough for most emergencies.

I didn't mind being left alone with Youn Hee for a day. I figured it would give her a chance to get used to me. We live in a development of about 150 houses off the county road near a big shopping mall. There's a small playground and lots of woods within walking distance of our house, so

Youn Hee and I would have enough to see and do.

"I'll check in with you around lunchtime. OK?" Mom asked.

"Fine."

I'd had a good night's sleep and a day to remind myself that Youn Hee had nothing and I had a lot. My confidence was back. My spirits were up. Your mission, I told myself, is to make Youn Hee smile.

Chapter Five

Youn Hee slept all evening, but when I woke up the next morning, she was sitting on the blanket on the floor beside the bed with the things from her case spread out around her. Item: one baggy, red, Korean-style dress with a yellow yoke. Also, a pair of white socks and underpants. Items: a bunch of short, fat sticks with a round side and a flat side, all the same length; a pink plastic hair-brush; a fan. Plus there was an official-looking envelope with Korean writing on it. She sat opening and closing the fan while she studied her belongings. They didn't look like much to me, and I wondered why she guarded them so carefully.

"Good morning, Youn Hee," I said.

Her eyes flew up at me. "Si Won?" She was asking for her brother.

"He's in the next room. Want me to show

you?" I led her to Simon, who was sleeping on his bare bed, clutching his green plush alligator to his chest. Mom must have covered him during the night because he had the afghan she'd knitted over him.

Youn Hee surveyed his room, which looked sort of like a store window display of a toy village without the electric train or the Christmas decorations. She gave a disapproving sniff, so I hurriedly explained, "He's into building," as if she could understand me. I knew she couldn't, but looking up the words in Korean would have taken too long.

Sunbeams were poking Simon's plump cheek. Youn Hee began poking at him, too, and talking to him in Korean. Her voice tinkled away like wind chimes. He woke up and stared at her as if he didn't remember who she was. Then he saw me and asked, "What's she want?"

"I don't know, but you've got to get up and go to school today, Simon."

He yawned widely and snuggled back down with his alligator.

"Simon, you miss the bus again and your friends will call you sleepyhead," I said.

He opened one eye. "My friends don't call me names. They're my *friends*."

"Then who called you sleepyhead last time?"

He sat up. "Nobody. Just Patti."

Youn Hee went into action then. She clapped her hands and tinkled faster.

"What's she saying?" Simon asked me in alarm.

"I don't know, but she seems to like you."

"Well, I gotta get dressed. Make her get out of my room."

I touched Youn Hee's arm and pointed the way. She glared at me and suddenly I saw the family resemblance. Their faces were different, but their anger looked the same. I shrugged and walked out of the room. Let Simon deal with his sister. She liked *him*.

I don't know what he did, but a minute later Youn Hee was back in my bedroom where I was getting dressed. She turned away from me and began repacking her bag.

Something smelled like cookies baking downstairs. I figured Youn Hee could follow her nose there or follow Simon, so I pointed to my stomach, said, "Eat," and left her.

Mom was in the kitchen, dressed for work. She had put out two kinds of cereal, a dish of raisins, and glasses of apple juice, orange juice, and milk. The sweet smell came from muffins she was taking out of the oven.

"I got up at dawn to make these," she said proudly. "From a mix, but they smell good, don't they?"

"Great," I said.

"How does she seem this morning?"

"Korean," I said.

"What do you mean?"

"Well, I can't even talk to her."

"*Umm.* The sooner she starts that intensive language training class at school the better. Maybe we'll take her to school tomorrow."

"You take her. She won't do anything for me."

"Caitlin, you're jumping to conclusions."

"She's not the least bit like I expected," I complained. Maybe I was making hasty judgments, which Mom says is my worst fault, but it really hurt that Youn Hee looked at me as if I were her enemy.

"Give her a chance, Caitlin. She just got here."

"I know." I sighed and resolved to be patient.

"Yum, muffins," Simon said. He was dressed for school with his sneakers on the wrong feet as usual. By the time I got him to switch them, Youn Hee had appeared in the clothes she'd worn when she came.

"Tonight we go to the mall and get her a wardrobe," Mom said. She smiled at Youn Hee and pointed to a seat at the kitchen table.

But before Youn Hee sat, she went over to Simon and with a little bow handed him the four sticks I'd seen on her blanket. She made a short speech in her chiming Korean. Then she pointed to herself and said clearly, *"Noo na."* When he didn't react, she pushed him a little and pointed to herself again and said the word.

"I thought her name was Youn Hee," I said to Mom. "Maybe it's Noo na. Maybe we got the wrong kid and that's why she's so little and doesn't like me."

"Caitlin, don't be ridiculous." Mom was paging through sheets of Korean vocabulary.

She must have been studying them while she was cooking.

"Noo na," Simon said when Youn Hee poked him the second time.

"Cha ka da," she told him with a big smile.

"I know what that means," I said. It was one of the phrases I still remembered from when Simon came. "Good boy. I think she wants you to call her Noo na, Simon."

"OK," he said. "But what'd she give me these sticks for?"

"They're probably meant as a gift," Mom said.

Simon made a face. He put the sticks, which were almost as thick as chair legs, down beside his cereal bowl and reached for his apple juice.

At least Noo na, or Youn Hee, was ready to eat this morning. She looked into the two cereal boxes Mom offered her and chose the rice squares. She ate them dry. I don't know how she did that. I need them soggy enough to swallow.

When Mom took Simon off to get the school bus, Noo na, or Youn Hee, looked alarmed even though Mom said good-bye in Korean and tried, in Korean, to explain they'd be back later. Youn Hee/Noo na's eyes fixed on me. She could see she was stuck with me, and *I* could see she didn't like that much. Then she noticed the four sticks Simon had left beside his plate. She bit her lip and tears filled her eyes. I guessed it was because Simon hadn't liked her gift.

"Don't cry, Noo na," I said. "He's only a little guy. He doesn't understand."

At that she burst into tears and ran back upstairs to the bedroom. Simon wasn't the only one who didn't understand. Not speaking their language really gets in the way of communicating with someone. That's for sure. I wondered if she'd like me better when she learned English, or if it was something about the way I looked that she hated. I was a giant compared to her, but I have an OK face, kind of friendly and open. And I have dimples. How can you hate anyone with dimples?

I went to work cleaning up the breakfast dishes, then got the little kid's picture dictionary from the box of discarded toys in the garage and took it upstairs to my bedroom. Youn Hee was standing beside the window peeking out as if she were a prisoner.

"Noo na," I began.

She whipped around and her eyes flashed at me as she snapped, "Youn Hee. I Youn Hee." She pointed to herself to make sure I got the message.

"Whew!" I said. "I'm glad you're Youn Hee. You had me confused there for a while. So anyway—Youn Hee—want to look at this book with me?" I smiled, flashing my dimples back at her.

I don't know if the dimples did it or what, but she calmed down and came over. She sat on the bed on the other side of the book, which I'd spread out between us, as if she didn't trust me any closer. It reminded me of once when I'd tried to make friends with an alley cat. Any movement and she'd skitter off.

"Apple," I said, pointing to the first picture.

After a few pages, naming things out loud got kind of boring, and I just nudged the book her way. She paged through it, then began at the beginning, and when she found something that interested her, she pointed at it. "Baby," I said.

"Baby," she repeated.

At last we had something going! I taught

her "dress" and "spoon" and "girl." We went on that way for so long I began yawning and losing interest, but she didn't. She kept me at it for over an hour. Finally I got up and beckoned her downstairs, where I flipped on the TV. She understood that right away, but there was nothing on in the morning that I wanted to watch, just talk shows and exercise and cooking shows.

I gave her a tour of the house, naming appliances and furniture and whatever. Her eyes kept going to the windows. Finally I asked her, "Walk, yes?" She questioned me with her eyes, and I pantomimed walking and pointed outside. "Walk, yes?"

She shrugged uncertainly. "No?" I said and shook my head.

"Yes," she said.

I gave her my winter jacket to wear, thinking it would work like a coat on her, but the sleeves hung down to her knees and I giggled at how goofy she looked. She frowned at me. I risked getting her really mad then by pushing her around to look at herself in the hall mirror. What a relief when she smiled at that orangutan fit. Anyone who can laugh at herself has possibilities in my book.

Mom had bought Simon a snow parka on sale that was still too big for him. It fit Youn Hee just fine. She checked herself out in the mirror again, and on came the smile. "Yes," she said. The parka was bright red and turquoise and yellow. Simon liked bright colors. I guess his sister did, too.

We walked side-by-side past all the deserted lawns and driveways. There weren't even any dog walkers or joggers out. Not that it was cold—forty degrees maybe—but there was a gray lid on the day. Little kids were indoors, and most everybody else was at school or work. I wondered what Youn Hee thought of our neighborhood. The houses were pretty much alike, just different colors of gray or white or blue in colonial or ranch style, with lots of tall trees the builder had left standing. Was this what she expected? Was it like Korea? I wished I knew how to ask her.

Trying to communicate with Youn Hee was exhausting me, and it was a relief to do something physical. I get energy from physical activities, especially fun ones like ball games. We walked to the neighborhood playground, which is in a green area separating our development from the medical offices next to it. The playground is mostly used by little kids.

"You can take Simon here," I told Youn Hee, but I don't think she understood me, although she might have. Later she admitted that she had started learning English in the orphanage before she knew she was coming to the United States, but she'd been too shy and scared to use it.

Anyway, she headed right for the swings and immediately got on one, not sitting but standing. I guess they must have swings in Korea because she knew what to do all right. She pumped herself high in the air with her head flung back and her straight black hair flipping out. She was enjoying herself so much that I got on the swing next to her and did some high flying myself.

"Cold?" I asked her when we'd slowed down. I pretended to shiver and asked again, "Cold?"

She shook her head, no. So we hung around the park, but she didn't seem that interested in the slides or the tire mountain or the tire bridge. She picked up a maple leaf that was still red even though it was late November. Her face got sad again and I was afraid she'd start crying. It was frustrating to have her be such a complete mystery to me.

"Eat?" I rubbed my stomach and pretended to put food in my mouth. "Yes?"

She laughed as if I were funny. "Yes," she said. We walked home side-by-side with me feeling a little better about how we were getting along.

Still, by the time Simon got home from school, I was glad to hand Youn Hee over to him. Trying to make her understand me was hard work. Not that she wasn't smart. She remembered a bunch of words already, and she was probably using the English words she'd learned in Korea. But there's a lot more than a bunch of words in a real conversation.

"Si Won," she said when he bopped through the door with his day's drawings and work sheets clutched in his hand. "Eat?"

"I'm Simon," he said, planting his feet and pointing to his own chest. "Simon, not Si Won."

I held my breath, thinking it might break her down again, but she repeated meekly, "Simon."

Simon turned to me. "I got three cookies

at snack time. Jared gave me his. See my planes? I made a whole bunch of planes."

I hugged him—my little brother! "Good work, Simon," I said.

Youn Hee watched us quietly. Now *she* must be feeling left out, I thought. And she was here alone. There was only one of her and three of us, Simon and Mom and me. I felt guilty to have him treating me like his sister and Youn Hee like a stranger.

"Simon," I said. "Show Youn Hee your work." And I pushed him toward her. If I'd known what was ahead of us, believe me, I wouldn't have.

Chapter Six

At dinner that night I made Youn Hee show off the words she'd learned, and Mom was really impressed. "I learn some Korea," Youn Hee said.

"Oh, you started learning English before you came?" Mom asked.

Youn Hee nodded. "Nevertheless," Mom said, "you're doing really well."

Mom's praise got such a big smile from Youn Hee that Simon said, "Hey, she's pretty!" as if he'd just noticed.

She was a little awkward eating the stir-fried chicken and vegetables with her fork, so I found a pair of chopsticks for her, which resulted in all of us trying to eat with chopsticks. Mom and I did OK, but Simon was really funny. He kept dropping his chicken even when he got his nose right down to his plate. Youn Hee didn't laugh at him with us though. In fact, she acted upset and kept trying to teach him in a sort of bossy way by fixing the chopsticks in his chubby fingers. No matter how she tried, he couldn't get the sticks to work right.

"Youn Hee, let him—," Mom began, just as Simon pushed Youn Hee's hands aside and said, "I don't like chopsticks. Forks are better."

We ate everything and had frozen yogurt for dessert. "Great dinner," I told Mom. It wasn't just the food, it was that we were eating together like the family I'd imagined us being. Youn Hee even got up and helped me clear the table. Simon, of course, escaped to the TV.

"So, are we ready for the big shopping trip?" Mom asked.

"Yes," I said, and Youn Hee echoed me, although I don't know if she knew what she was agreeing to.

I took my money along, thinking that after we'd gotten Youn Hee some clothes I could take her to a bookstore or toy store and find her a good welcome-to-the-family gift from me.

Our first stop was a children's clothing store. Mom started trying to figure out Youn

Hee's size, while Youn Hee was busy swallowing the place whole with her eyes as if she'd never seen anything like it. Probably she hadn't. The store was packed floor to ceiling with displays of children's clothes. Anyway, Mom collected an armload of pants and skirts and tops, and she took Youn Hee to the dressing room.

I was supposed to be in charge of Simon. He was marching his monster-into-robot transformer along the floor when Mom beckoned me into the dressing room, so I left him for a minute.

"I can't figure out what she likes," Mom said. "She says yes to everything."

"Maybe she likes everything."

"Well, fine, but I can't afford it all. You help her select a couple of pairs of pants and a skirt and a few tops, Caitlin. I'll watch Simon."

Youn Hee had on a sweater that looked like a sleeping bag on her.

"Yes?" she said.

"No." I shook my head and tried to act out "too big." She giggled.

I showed her a smaller sweater and she put that on. "Yes?" I said.

"No." She shook her head hard. I couldn't

63

guess what she didn't like, but she definitely didn't like that sweater. We'd found a few items of clothing that we both "yessed," when all of a sudden I heard Mom screeching Simon's name.

I ran out into the store. A man with a squinched-up face was holding Simon by the back of his shirt. Simon had a fistful of tickets—the kind they hang on clothes to tell you the size and price.

"He went through the whole rack," the man was complaining to Mom, "every item. Do you know how many hours it'll take to reticket those garments, lady?"

"I'm terribly sorry," Mom said. "I'm sure he didn't mean—"

"You need to learn to control your kids."

Mom stopped looking apologetic at that. "Simon's only five years old," she said.

"Exactly, and he shouldn't be running around unsupervised."

Mom raised an eyebrow at the grouchy man and opened her mouth to say something, but Youn Hee had followed me out of the dressing room and now she got in on the act. She yelled at Simon in Korean, which was OK because he didn't understand what she was saying, but when he didn't answer her, she hit him. She just smacked him right across the face.

Mom gasped. "Youn Hee! Oh dear." Immediately Mom grabbed Simon and Youn Hee each by an arm and ushered them out of the store.

"What about the stuff we picked?" I asked. "Want to give me the money and I'll go back and buy it?"

"You can't sign for my credit card," Mom said. "Anyway, I'm not buying a thing in that man's store. Why is he selling children's clothing if he doesn't like children?"

"But, Mom, Simon was bad."

Grudgingly, Mom agreed to that. She even said, "Simon, you must never do anything like that again, you hear?"

In answer, he puffed himself up and pointed at Youn Hee. "But she hit me."

"Well, she was upset because you were naughty and she's your sister."

"She's *not* my sister," he protested. "She's Korean. I'm American like Caitlin."

"We're both your sisters," I said.

"No, she's not my sister." He folded his arms across his chest and moved as far away from Youn Hee as he could get.

"I don't know," Mom muttered. "Maybe

I'm too old for this motherhood business.
. . . Come on, let's try the department
store. They have children's clothing."

That was when I noticed Youn Hee's
face. It was so sad it made me want to cry.
"She doesn't understand, Mom," I said. "I
bet she thinks you're punishing her by not
buying her those clothes."

"Youn Hee," Mom said. "It's all right.
We'll get you clothes, just not at that store,
OK? Come. You're a good girl." She stroked
Youn Hee's sleek black hair to reassure her,
but she added, "Except you shouldn't smack
Simon like that."

"Mom, she doesn't understand *that* much
English yet, does she?"

Mom groaned. "Of course she doesn't.
Listen, tomorrow you *all* go to school. The
sooner she starts in that intensive language
training program the better." She marched
ahead of us with Simon's hand in hers, making him trot to keep up with her.

Meanwhile, I took Youn Hee's hand and
smiled at her. "Don't worry," I said. "It'll
be OK." I wasn't sure she understood that,
either. I was doing just what Mom had done,
talking at her too fast with too many words.

It occurred to me that if I was weary from trying to communicate with her all day, she must be really worn out from a whole day of trying to understand.

We tugged her along to the other end of the mall, where we found children's clothing in the back of the department store.

This time Mom knew the right size. She wanted Youn Hee to try on a bunch of things again to see if she liked them, but Youn Hee showed no interest.

"Look, Youn Hee." I held out a cute shirt with pink-and-purple musical notes on it. "Nice? Yes?"

She kept her head down and wouldn't answer.

Finally Mom picked out a bunch of clothes for her and some underwear. "She needs another pair of sneakers," Mom said. "Do you think we can get her to put *them* on?"

"I don't know."

"Well, let's try," Mom said. "I'm not up for another trip to the mall anytime soon."

The shoe salesman did his best. He kept chatting up Youn Hee, who slumped in the chair, limp as a rag doll. "Now what color sneakers would a pretty little girl like you want?" he asked her. I told him she didn't speak English yet. Mom had already explained that, but I guess he couldn't believe it. Like if *he* spoke English, everybody had to understand it.

"Pink's a good color." He pointed to pink-and-white sneakers. "Do you like pink, little lady?"

Youn Hee ignored him. Her face was set as if she wasn't about to be tricked into smiling again.

"Get her plain white sneakers like mine. They go with everything," I said.

"Right," Mom said.

Youn Hee let the salesman lift her foot, but when he took off her sneaker, she jerked back and cried out.

"You better give her back her shoe," I said. "She probably thinks you're going to steal it."

She clung to the old sneaker as he fitted on a new pair that Mom said she'd buy.

"Whew," the salesman said. "Toughest sale I had all day. Most kids love getting new sneakers."

"She will, too, as soon as she believes

they're hers," I told him. I figured pulling her away from the clothes in the first store had convinced her that we were just teasing her and weren't going to let her keep anything.

"Where's Simon?" Mom asked after she'd given the salesman her charge card.

I looked around. We'd been concentrating so hard on buying sneakers that we'd lost track of him again.

"Caitlin," Mom said, "I thought you were watching him."

"Well, I was, but so were you. Weren't you, Mom?"

She just groaned.

We found him calmly sucking a lollipop and kicking his heels against the service desk. "We were just about to page you," the lady who was keeping him for us said. "Real cute little boy."

Simon beamed up at me angelically while Mom thanked the customer service lady and herded us out to the car. I handed Youn Hee her bag of clothes and the bag with the sneakers as soon as we were sitting in the back of the car. She looked puzzled.

"They're yours," I said pointing.

"I?"

"Yes," I nodded.

"Yes?" She hugged the bag of clothes to her chest then, but she didn't start smiling again. In fact, she still seemed sad.

"What's the matter with her, Mom?" I asked later. I'd finished reading to Simon and sent him off to sleep, and Mom had just gotten downstairs from supervising Youn Hee's bath and tucking her into my bed.

"Probably just that she doesn't know what's going on," Mom said. "Or maybe she's disappointed that Simon isn't more Korean. After all, the last time she saw him, he spoke her language and no doubt behaved himself a whole lot better than he does now. I'm not doing a very good job of taming him, Caitlin. That man in the store had a point. What Simon needs is a full-time mother . . . and a father no doubt. . . . I may not have done these two any favor when I agreed to adopt them."

"You're just overtired, Mom," I said. "You always get the glooms when you're tired, remember? You better take a hot bath and go to bed early."

Mom laughed and ruffled my hair. "Sounds like familiar advice."

"Well, it's good advice, and I learned it from a great mom."

"Oh, Caitlin," Mom said. "It's your fault I took on these two. You made being a mother seem easy because you're such a good kid."

"I thought I was too quick to judge and impatient and a lousy student."

"Minor flaws in an otherwise perfect child," Mom said. She hugged me and rocked me in her arms.

Youn Hee was actually *on* the bed when I climbed over her to the window side. "Hey," I said, "so are you glad you came?" But she shut her eyes and turned her back to me. Spending a day together hadn't made her trust me any more. We were still strangers as far as she was concerned. Too bad, but she didn't have anybody except Simon and Mom and me. No matter how she felt, I had better keep trying to be her sister because, whether she liked it or not, she *needed* me.

Chapter Seven

Audrey pounced on me in homeroom the next morning. "So what's she like? I tried to call you last night, but you weren't home."

"We were out shopping," I said. Bud, Denise, and Avery, a tall skinny kid who plays basketball with us sometimes, shoved their desks closer to mine to hear my answer. I guess Youn Hee had become a hot news item, but I didn't want to sound negative and I couldn't be that positive, so I just said, "The thing is, she doesn't speak much English."

"But is she going to be in our class?" Denise asked.

"I don't know," I said. "Mom's down in guidance with her right now."

"So do you like her? Does she have fangs?" Audrey persisted.

"Hey, lay off, Audrey," I said. "I don't know yet."

They looked disappointed, which made me feel worse. Sharing the sticky stuff with each other is what makes us friends, and I wasn't sharing.

"I guess it's hard when she doesn't speak English," Bud said. Trust Bud to let me off the hook.

To my relief, homeroom started then and we had to be quiet. I sat there gnawing away at Audrey's question. The truth was Youn Hee did show signs of having "fangs," judging by the way she'd hit Simon last night and her bossiness about the chopsticks. He might be her brother, but she didn't know him yet, so what right did she have to try and change him? Besides, Simon was fun and it didn't seem that Youn Hee would ever be. I took a deep breath, telling myself I'd been the one most eager to adopt her and since we couldn't mail her back, I had to make the best of it.

At lunchtime Ms. Lane, our ancient guidance counselor, she of the dandelion fluff hair, braved the zoo—otherwise known as the student cafeteria—to deliver Youn Hee to my table.

"I thought you might want to show your new sister the ropes here, Caitlin," Ms. Lane said to me. "I expect she needs a familiar face."

"Oh, sure." I shoved over, nudging Audrey to the end of the bench and making room for Youn Hee next to me.

"After she's eaten, would you bring her back to my office, please?"

"Sure," I said again.

Ms. Lane bobbed off through the noise, and I began trying to introduce Youn Hee to my friends. I pointed at freckle-faced, long-nosed Audrey and said her name. "Say it, Youn Hee," I told her.

"Audey," she whispered.

"Hi, Youn Hee," Audrey said with a big grin. To me, she said, "She looks like a little Chinese doll."

"I Korean," Youn Hee said loud and clear.

"I thought she didn't speak English," Audrey protested.

"She learns fast," I said.

We got through the names, and then I steered Youn Hee to the food counter. I showed her some sandwiches, but she shook her head. She didn't want the hot dish either, which I couldn't blame her for because it was upchuck chicken in a gooey white sauce. By the time we reached the cashier's station, Youn Hee had only said yes to an apple.

"My goodness, is that all you're going to eat for lunch, honey? No wonder you're so little," our grandmotherly cashier said.

"She's saving her lunch money for a plane ticket home," I said. Just making conversation, but the cashier took me seriously.

"Where does she come from? Japan?"

"Korea," I said before Youn Hee could.

"She's going to have to go without a lot of lunches to make it back there, won't she?"

That reminded me all over again of how scared and strange Youn Hee must feel so far from home. We probably even looked strange to her. Most people in the pictures I'd seen of Korea looked Korean, and in this cafeteria out of maybe 150 kids, there were no more than a dozen who looked Asian. I snatched up a couple of chocolate chip cookies, paid for them myself, and led Youn Hee back to our table.

"These are good," I said, putting the cookies down in front of her. "Yum." I licked my lips.

Audrey snickered at my performance. Denise leaned over and quietly gave Youn Hee her bag of potato chips. Bud said to me, "Let her be. She probably feels too homesick to eat."

"Homesick? But she lived in an orphanage," Audrey said.

"So? She knew people there, didn't she?" Bud asked.

Youn Hee was just sitting there not touching anything, not even the apple. Suddenly, I didn't like myself much. I'd been concentrating on how Youn Hee made me feel instead of how she must be feeling. On impulse, I put my arm around her and said, "Her home's here now."

She flinched and pulled away from me. My friends all looked at me like—"Have you been pinching her when nobody was watching?" I was crushed.

Usually we run outside to play soccer for the last twenty minutes of the period. That day, my friends stayed at the table with Youn Hee and me. I knew they'd rather chase a ball than sit and talk, so I appreciated that they stayed. Anyway, while Youn Hee nibbled at her apple and stared at them as if they were a puzzle she had to figure out, they talked at her.

"Korea nice?" Bud asked her.

"Yes," she said promptly.

"Caitlin nice," Bud said. "Your sister." He pointed to me.

Over the apple, Youn Hee's eyes fixed on me. She didn't say yes. I cringed. Why didn't she like me? Maybe I hadn't been sensitive to how she was feeling, but I was trying hard.

"Do you play ball?" Denise asked next.

Youn Hee said, "I no understand."

I was impressed that she'd produced a whole English sentence. "I bet she learned that just this morning," I said. Then I remembered she had said she started learning English before she found out she was coming to America.

"I'll show you what I mean, Youn Hee," Denise said, and she got out her notebook and started to draw. Did I mention that Denise is good at art, too?

"You have a brother?" Bud asked.

"Brother?" Youn Hee said. "Si Won."

"You mean Simon," Bud said. He smiled at her. "I have three brothers." He held up three fingers.

"Three?" Youn Hee said.

"Three," he said. "Two step- and one regular."

"Boy, Bud can talk to her already," Audrey said. "How long do you think she'll take to really speak English?"

"What's she speaking now, Audrey, Korean?" Bud asked.

"Well, you know what I mean." Audrey was speaking to me.

"I don't know," I said. "Maybe a year. After all, we've been doing it for more than ten and there are still words we don't know."

Denise had drawn a neat picture of a soccer game. She showed it to Youn Hee. "Ball," Denise said, pointing. "You play ball?"

"No." Youn Hee shook her head. Everybody at the table gaped.

"Well," I said, "we can teach her. You *want* to play ball, don't you, Youn Hee?" I urged.

"No." She shook her head with determination. "No play. No time."

"So what?" I said into their silence. "Everybody doesn't have to be the same, do they?" But I was as shaken as they were. How was I going to live with a sister who didn't have time to chase a ball around?

After lunch I rushed Youn Hee upstairs to the guidance office and bumped right into our principal, Mr. Pollock.

"Where are you going in such a hurry, Caitlin?" he demanded, stopping me in my tracks with his hooded-cobra glare.

"Guidance," I said. "I'm not doing a thing you can give me detention for, Mr. Pollock. Here." I picked up the pen he'd dropped when he spotted me and returned it to him. That wasn't why he looked so pained though. Mr. Pollock hates me. He's hated me ever since someone put sugar in the gas tank of his car last year. What happened was he saw me admiring the car and was sure I'd been up to mischief again, but just because I fool around sometimes doesn't mean I'm a bad kid. He grilled me in his office for an hour to make me confess, but I wouldn't because I was innocent. Only he wouldn't believe it. He even made Mom come to school. She said she trusted me, so he had to let me go, but he still thinks I did it. Most kids like Mr. Pollock. Well, if he didn't glare at me all the time, I probably would, too.

"Who that man?" Youn Hee asked me after Mr. Pollock finished telling me to be more careful, and we were on the way to the guidance office again.

"He's the principal," I said. "He runs the school. His name's Mr. Pollock."

I don't think Youn Hee understood what I'd said, but she asked, "He mean?"

"Just to me, Youn Hee," I said. "If you're good, you don't have to worry."

"I good," she said firmly.

"Yeah," I said. "I bet you are."

I had basketball practice after school. What I usually did was pick up Simon from his all-day kindergarten class and let him run around the stands in the gym by himself while he waited for me to take him home on the late bus. He was pretty good about it because I gave him a lollipop with a Toot-sie Roll center afterward if he'd stayed in the gym.

That day I had Youn Hee to collect, too. I herded them both across the glassy-finished wood floor to the shaky fold-up stands.

"You bringing in the whole kindergarten class to watch us now, Caitlin?" Mr. Hatch asked me. He's our bald, bow-legged basketball coach and gym teacher.

"Youn Hee just got here from Korea, but she's not a kindergartner. She's eleven," I said. "She'll behave."

"Yeah? Well, see to it your little brother does, too. No more jumping around the stands. He sits, or he's out."

"OK, Coach." I sat Simon down and Youn Hee parked herself beside him. "See if you can explain the game to her, Simon," I said.

"OK." Simon's confidence tickled me because he doesn't know what's going on himself.

As soon as I began trying to fake out Audrey, who was supposed to be guarding me, I forgot I had my own private audience. I got fouled twice and scored on two of my free throws. Simon cheered, but I was too busy dribbling the ball down the court to look up and see what Youn Hee was doing. Audrey got the ball away from me. I got it back and passed to Denise, who made a basket on a rebound. Then I tried for one and made it. The coach even complimented me after the game. "Nice playing, Caitlin." That meant a lot coming from him. But when I looked for Youn Hee and Simon, the stands were empty.

"Where'd they go?" I asked anxiously.

"They're probably waiting for you somewhere, Caitlin," Denise said. "Don't worry. They can't get lost."

"They can't?" I wasn't too sure about that. I checked the bathrooms, barging into both the boys' and girls'—well, it was after school hours. Nobody was in either bathroom.

I ran to the late bus. They were inside it, calmly watching my panicked behavior through the window.

"Hey," I said when I plopped into the seat across from them. "What'd you go off without telling me for? You scared me half to death."

"I found the bus," Simon said proudly.

"Simon, when you're supposed to wait someplace for me, you can't go wait someplace else. I'm responsible for you, remember?"

"But Youn Hee's with me."

"Yeah, well, she doesn't know anything yet," I said.

"She's my big sister, too. You said."

I didn't like it, but how could I argue with him?

Youn Hee's eyes switched back and forth from Simon to me. I couldn't very well blame her. She didn't even know what I was angry about. "Promise you won't go off without telling me again, Simon," I said.

"I promise." He said it too easily, the way he does to shut me up when he doesn't believe he's done anything wrong.

We got home and I unlocked the door. Simon was too young to have his own key and Mom hadn't given Youn Hee one yet. Until Youn Hee knew how to get around, I was responsible for her, too. I felt top-heavy just thinking about it.

Simon and I headed for the refrigerator. Youn Hee followed. She must have been really hungry because she ate a fruit yogurt and tried the peanut butter on crackers that Simon was eating, finishing up with cookies.

"Why can she get three and not me?" Simon wanted to know.

"Because she's older," I said.

"She wants me to call her Noo na."

"Yeah, so?"

"So how come you call her Youn Hee?"

"Don't ask me, Simon. When she can speak English, she'll tell us."

"I speak some," Youn Hee said unexpectedly.

"I know," I said. "I wish I knew how much though."

"*Noo na* is old sister," Youn Hee said suddenly. "You"—she pointed at me—"not say, *uhn nee,* old sister me." She pointed at herself.

"OK, so I'm your same sister," I said. "Or I will be after—if you get adopted. I mean, we have to wait six months, right?" I was being awkward. She had me so confused. Did she mean she didn't want to be my sister? Maybe she'd decide to go back to the orphanage. Could she take Simon with her? I got chills just thinking that.

"Simon," I said. "I'm your old sister, but you don't have to call me Noo na. Just keep calling me, Caitlin, OK?"

"OK."

"Simon, do you love me?" I asked him.

He pouted his lips out and thought about it. And do you know what the little twerp answered me? "Sometimes," he said.

I growled at him, "Well, I love you and I want you to keep on being my little brother, understand?"

At that he popped off his chair, threw his arms around my neck, and gave me a wet kiss that left his milk mustache on my cheek. I loved it, wet mustache and all, but when I glanced at Youn Hee, her eyes were narrowed and she looked upset. Tough, I thought, he's been my brother for three years.

I was on the phone for a long time with Bud, who tried to explain to me how to set up equations for our math homework. When I went looking for Simon and Youn Hee, they weren't watching TV where I'd left them. They were up in Simon's room sitting on the floor on a blanket, and Youn Hee was throwing those fat sticks she'd given him. Four fat sticks about six inches long. They landed with three rounded sides up and one flat side down. She said something in Korean and moved a paper marker over a couple of circles on a homemade board.

"What's going on?" I asked Simon.

"Noo na's teaching me a game," he said.

She beamed, looking happier than I'd seen her look yet. "Yes, Si Won, I Noo na," she said.

"Can I play, too?" I asked.

"Sure," Simon said. He hitched over to make room on the blanket for me. Youn Hee's smile dimmed when I joined them. It was more than language and ball games that would keep us from being sisters if Youn Hee just didn't like me. Well, I wasn't wild about her, either.

Chapter Eight

Mom was impressed with how fast Youn Hee was picking up English. Mom was impressed with a lot of things about Youn Hee.

For one thing, by the second week in December she had trained Simon to put his toys away. All of a sudden you could walk into his room without stepping on things. Mom always checked our rooms to make sure we hadn't left too discouraging a mess when the cleaning service people were due to come. One night she did a pre-cleaning service pick-up check and returned to the living room looking dazzled.

"How did you get Simon to pick up after himself, Youn Hee? Or are you doing it for him?" she asked.

"He does," Youn Hee said.

"You are amazing," Mom told her. "Caitlin and I gave up on him long ago."

"He must learn," Youn Hee said. And to my disgust, Mom nodded respectfully without asking how. For all she knew Youn Hee could be beating Simon up to persuade him to be good. Not that she was. I saw how she did it. Anyway, I think I did.

It was an afternoon when the rain had stopped. I went to ask Simon to kick the ball around outside with me and found Youn Hee sitting straight-backed on Simon's bed.

"No, Si Won," she was saying, "pick up now and we play more."

"I'll pick up later," he said.

She didn't budge. Just kept sitting. Simon coaxed, "Play marbles with me, Noo na. Please!" She wasn't hearing him. "You're mean, Noo na," he said. I would have started arguing with him then—and lost per usual. Youn Hee just perched, still as a bird on a power line, while he fussed and rolled out his lips and folded his arms and stamped his foot. Nothing he did or said moved her.

Finally Simon gave in. "OK, but you got to help me put the stuff away," he told her.

"I help you this time," she said. "Next time by yourself. . . . You have many toys, Si Won. Boys in Korea not have so many toys. You are lucky. Must take care of things."

"Simon," I said then from the doorway, "want to go outside and play soccer?"

He considered. "Not now, Caitlin. I must clean up my room."

That *must* really got to me. It was Youn Hee's favorite word. She *must* help with the dishes, do her homework, read to Simon, write letters to her friends at the orphanage. The first time I'd noticed her using it was after our disaster of a shopping trip, the day her bed was finally delivered. Youn Hee had bowed to Mom after dinner and said as formally as if she'd rehearsed it, "I must thank you for clothes and nice things. Thank you for new bed, also."

Maybe it was the word *must* that gave me the impression she was thanking Mom out of duty, but it did seem to me Youn Hee wasn't that thrilled to be here. I wondered why she'd come. One night when we were in bed, I even asked her.

"I come for Si Won," she had said. It scared me speechless.

Our baby-sitter, Hettie, didn't make me feel any more confident. She was at our house when I got home from a basketball game one evening. Mom didn't let Youn Hee take care of Simon alone because something could go wrong and Youn Hee might not know what to do, so Hettie still sat for us often. Anyway, Mom was asking Hettie how much she owed her, and Hettie pursed her wrinkled face and said, "I really shouldn't take anything. All I do is sit here knitting while Youn Hee takes charge of Simon. It's remarkable the way he listens to that little bitty girl. He sure knows she's his big sister."

Christmas decorations were up all over town. Our neighbors had wreaths on their doors and electric candles in the windows, all except Hettie, who's Jewish. The bushes and trees of the house across the street were blooming with colored lights. Someone had a big red-and-white lighted Santa Claus on their front lawn. The streets around us glittered and twinkled at night. But Mom's not much for seasonal decorating. She stuck our old pinecone wreath with its frumpy red velvet ribbon on the front door and dug our fake tree out of the back of the garage. I groaned so loudly when I saw it again that she agreed to get a real one this year instead.

At dinner that night I mentioned to Mom that we ought to go to the mall. "We need new tree lights. Besides, I never got Youn Hee the welcome gift I was going to buy her," I said.

"No need," Youn Hee tinkled immediately. "No, thank you."

I felt like she'd slapped me.

It wasn't Youn Hee's night to help with the dishes. After the chocolate pudding, she asked to be excused so she could go upstairs and read with Simon. Mom was glad to let her go because she thought it was good practice for Youn Hee to read to Simon.

"I guess she doesn't want a gift from me," I said to Mom as I dried the pots she'd scrubbed.

"Oh, I'm sure she didn't mean that, Caitlin. Don't be so sensitive."

"She doesn't like me."

I'd told Mom that before, but she'd said I was imagining things and that I should be patient. Tonight what Mom said was, "Caitlin, are you sure you don't feel that way because *you* don't like *her?*"

"I like her OK."

"Do you? You certainly don't like sharing Simon with her. You get your back up every time Youn Hee does something alone with him."

"I do not," I protested.

"What about last night when they were playing Candyland? You told him that was a baby game and you'd teach him a big kid's card game."

"Well, I would have taught Youn Hee, too."

"It's natural to be jealous, sweetie. Just don't let it get the best of you," Mom said.

"But he always chooses her!" I complained, surprising myself because I didn't know I had that much whine in me.

"Simon still loves you, Caitlin. You know people do have multiple siblings and love them all, each for different reasons," Mom said.

"Only she thinks that Simon's *really* her brother. He's just adopted with me."

"Caitlin"—Mom put her arm around me and hugged me—"are you feeling left out?"

I knew admitting that I did made me sound like a baby, but I couldn't help myself.

"I *am* left out," I grumbled. "When she plays games with Simon, they don't invite me, and if I ask if I can play, too, she doesn't like it, Mom."

"Maybe you should remind yourself that you have a lot, and Youn Hee has nothing— just one little brother. If she's possessive about him, it's understandable, isn't it?"

"I don't care. He's my brother, too. Didn't adopting Simon make him as much my brother as if he were born into our family?"

"Technically it does. That is, it's supposed to. Oh, I don't know," Mom said. "Just keep being the generous, kind girl you've always been, and it will work out. I'm sure it will."

But a couple of nights later I came out of the bathroom after taking my bath and heard Mom and Simon and Youn Hee laughing together down in the living room. I ran downstairs in my pajamas to join in the fun. They were playing that Korean game with the sticks—*yout* is what it's called. Mom invited me to join them and I did, but Youn Hee didn't like having to explain the game to me, and Simon and Mom kept giving me confusing instructions. I couldn't get it and I felt so stupid I gave up and went to bed. They kept playing as if they didn't notice me leaving. Even Mom. I was the outsider, me, not Youn Hee, who hadn't even been with our family a month.

"You think she's a perfect little darling, don't you, Mom?" I accused my mother the next morning.

"I think Youn Hee's a good little girl who's trying very hard. This country is strange to her and we're strange to her, and she doesn't have a mother or father to turn to."

"But what about me? I'm trying hard, too."

"Of course you are, Caitlin, and I know you'll keep trying, won't you?" Mom hugged me and planted a kiss on my nose, but I pulled away.

"Yeah, yeah, yeah," I said. I was thinking it was easy enough for Mom to see the big picture. She was the adult, and she wasn't home all day, and she didn't have to share everything with Youn Hee like I did. OK, I'd keep trying, but I didn't like it.

I didn't like myself very much either because I knew I wasn't being generous *or* kind. It disappointed me to find out I was just an ordinary rotten kid when I'd always thought I was basically good-hearted.

Chapter Nine

The bus incident happened two weeks before Christmas vacation. Some boys grabbed a knitted tam from an eighth-grade girl sitting on the seat in front of Youn Hee and me. The driver stopped the bus and got the hat back, but he couldn't make the boys admit they'd taken it.

"Bad boys," Youn Hee said. "In Korea they get punished."

"Why? They were just teasing," I said.

"To make boys behave is more better," she said. "In Korea boys don't do bad things like here."

"You liked Korea better, didn't you?" I asked.

She hesitated. "I like here," she said cautiously. "But Si Won needs spanking. He don't get it here."

"Why does he need a spanking? He hasn't done anything awful lately."

She bit her lower lip and her eyes slid at me and away. I guessed Simon had done something, and she didn't trust me enough to tell me about it. Instead she assured me smugly, "I make Si Won be good."

Somehow that got me so mad that I said, "Listen, Youn Hee, Simon's your brother, but he's my brother, too. Even if you don't want to be my sister, he's my brother, understand?" I was shaking and unbelievably close to tears. Me, who boasts no one can make me cry!

We didn't talk to each other for the rest of the bus ride. We even avoided sitting near each other on the bus in the days that followed. Youn Hee sat alone, and I sat with any kid I knew who had an empty seat to share. We didn't have much to do with each other in the house, either. It's amazing how much distance you can put between yourself and someone you live with.

The week before Christmas vacation, Simon got in big trouble in school.

Youn Hee was in my classes when she wasn't in intensive language training, so when the messenger from the kindergarten asked for Simon's sister, both of us stood up. Our teacher looked from one to the other of us and hesitated as if she couldn't decide who was the real sister. Finally she sent us both down to the kindergarten, where Simon was leading a one-man war. His teacher had taken everyone out to recess, leaving her aide in the room alone with Simon. He was standing in the middle of a low, round table with a devilish look in his eye, swinging chukka sticks over his head—you know, the sticks with clublike ends that're used in karate. I could see how even a teacher wouldn't want to get near those things.

"Hey, Simon, you won the war. It's time to make peace," I said. I don't think he heard me because Youn Hee was screeching at him in Korean. Little and delicate as she was, she made him flinch when she went over and walloped him one on the rear end. After the shopping mall incident, Mom had told her we don't smack people in the face. Or maybe since Simon was on the table, Youn Hee couldn't reach his face, but anyway, she sure wasn't worried that he might hit her with those clubs.

"What were you doing with those sticks, Simon?" I asked after Youn Hee took them away from him and handed them over to the aide.

"I'm the karate kid," Simon said proudly.

"You bad, bad boy," Youn Hee told him.

"But he knocked down my village and then he called me names."

"Who did?"

"Michael. So I took the sticks he brought for show-and-tell."

"What names?" I asked.

"Slant-eye yellow shrimp."

"So call him round-eye pale ape," I said.

The aide didn't say a word. She just marched the three of us down to the principal's office. When I saw where we were heading, I said, "I'll just let Youn Hee and Simon deal with this and go on back to class, OK?"

"You come along, too," the aide said, kind of grim-faced.

"But I'll just make things worse for Si-mon," I said. And in case she didn't know, I confided, "See, the principal hates me."

She sniffed and kept walking. What could I do? I hummed the funeral march to myself and followed.

Mr. Pollock was busy, so the secretary told us to wait on the bad kids' bench outside the fenced office area. Youn Hee looked close to tears. "Don't worry," I told her. "It's too close to Christmas for the principal to do anything awful to Simon."

"I worry he's bad," Youn Hee said. "Bad, bad. In Korea you not stand on table in class and hit kids. Teacher not let you."

"So what would he do in Korea? Be a wimp?"

"No. He re-spek. He *ressspek* his teacher. He grow up right."

"In an orphanage?"

"No," Youn Hee said. Tears came to her eyes. "No, no." She bit her lip and wrung her hands. "No orphanage for Si Won, but—"

All of a sudden I felt sorry for her. "Si-mon'll grow up all right here," I said. "He's only five years old, Youn Hee. He has a lot to learn."

"In Korea they not call him names," Youn Hee said. Her eyes were flashing, and I realized the names had upset her more than anything.

"The names don't mean anything, Youn Hee," I said. "Pointing out what's different about you's no big deal because everybody's different in America."

"I'm not yellow. I'm vanilla, like you, Caitlin," Simon said.

"You're tan," I said. "A beautiful, strong, tan boy."

"Girls're beautiful, not boys," Simon protested.

"All right then. You're a handsome, strong, tan boy."

"Yes," Simon agreed. He sat back as if he was pleased with himself. He did seem to be until the principal read him the riot act and told him that was no way to behave in school. Simon was to apologize to his teacher and stay in from recesses for a week. The punishment made Simon gulp and look guilty. For a minute anyway.

As for me, all Mr. Pollock asked was, "These two related to you?"

"Yes," I said. "But they can't help it."

"Just don't teach them any of your tricks," he said.

"What tricks? Mr. Pollock, I'm a sixth-grader now. I don't leave dead mice on the teacher's chair anymore. . . . And I *didn't* put sugar in your gas tank. I didn't. Please, won't you believe me?"

The hooded eyes stared at me so expressionlessly I didn't have a clue what he was thinking.

"Whew, that was close," I said when we'd been released and were back in the hall.

Youn Hee let out the breath she must have been holding the whole time we were in the office. She hadn't said a word in there, I realized. "Did he scare you, Youn Hee?" I asked.

"Yes," she said.

"He didn't scare me," Simon said.

At that Youn Hee let loose at him with what sounded like a first-rate scolding in

Korean. When she'd run out of charge, he asked me, "What did she say?"

"I don't know. But you better apologize, Simon."

"I'm sorry," he said. "I'm sorry, Noo na."

"You be sorry, too, Caitlin," Youn Hee turned on me to say. "You the one teach Simon to be bad. You—you teach him fight with kids and talk big to grown-ups and make them mad. You should respek grown-ups, but you don't. And you make Simon not respek, either. And you—you. Oh!" She stuck her knuckle in her mouth and bit it in frustration.

"Youn Hee," I said. "Youn Hee—" But it was hard to defend myself because she was right in a way. I mean, my big mouth did get me in trouble with adults, and I did lose control sometimes and get physical to solve problems. Was I a bad example to Simon? The idea shocked me.

After dinner I helped Simon draw a picture for his teacher of a boy with tears running down his cheeks to show how sorry he was. When I went up to my bedroom, Youn Hee was writing a letter. She looked over her shoulder and her kitten face was spiteful as she said, "I tell my friend Hee Sook I come back to Korea."

"Really? When are you leaving?"

"Soon. When spring come, I go back. Si Won, too."

"You think an orphanage is better than here?"

Her expression changed. She looked uncertain. But anyway, I had already checked out that possibility with Mom. "You can't take Simon to an orphanage, Youn Hee. We've adopted him. He belongs to us."

"No. He belong *me!*" She screamed it so fiercely that I didn't argue with her. But the next morning I double-checked with Mom again.

"Don't worry. It could never happen," Mom told me soothingly. "Youn Hee was probably just upset. Her brother's behavior reflects on her, you know. If he's bad, she loses face. Remember the first time we took her shopping, and he pulled off those tickets and she slapped him?"

"And then she was upset because we didn't buy the clothes in that store."

"My guess is she was upset because of her brother's behavior."

I thought about it. Mom could be right. I sighed. "Youn Hee's so Korean," I said.

"And what's wrong with that?"

"I didn't used to think there was anything wrong with it," I said. "But I'm not so sure anymore. Simon's American, but I don't think Youn Hee will ever be."

"Can you only get along with Americans?"

"Getting along is one thing, Mom. Being a family is another."

For once Mom didn't try to correct me.

Chapter Ten

Simon only lost one recess before he got sick. Mom had to stay home from work with him Friday. But from the time Youn Hee and I got home from school Friday afternoon until Tuesday when he was well enough to go back to kindergarten, Simon ruled the house. He thought Youn Hee and I were his slaves and, boy, did that little twerp run us around!

"Play with me . . . I'm thirsty . . . I want ice cream . . . I want chocolate milk . . . I need an ice cube to suck . . . I need tissue . . . Read to me . . . I'm sick."

I got pretty sick of waiting on him and began dragging my heels when he asked for anything, but Youn Hee never stopped running. She got the better sister award if being a good sister means spoiling a kid rotten.

"Oh, lord and master, brother Simon,

what is thy will?" I intoned, kneeling beside his bed Monday afternoon after Hettie had gone home.

He studied me warily. "Play go fish with me?"

"Go fish," I said and grabbed my throat and stuck out my tongue. "Oh, not again, master. No! No go fish."

Simon chuckled. He thought I was pretty funny, and since he was feeling better, he stuck a bare foot out of his bed and stepped on my leg as I knelt there beside him. "Get the cards," he said and kicked me. "You got to listen to me."

I stood up. "Not anymore, kid. You're well. You get your own cards."

I glanced over my shoulder and saw Youn Hee had come into the room. I expected her to hop to and offer to get the cards. Instead she said, "Simon, you go take bath. To-morrow you go to school."

"Who says?"

"Mommy says."

It was the first time I'd heard her refer to our mother as Mommy, and besides that I had heard her say Simon instead of Si Won. Was there a crack in the Korean wall?

Next to Simon's bed was a box of origami airplanes and hats and boxes and animals that Youn Hee had spent hours making for him on Sunday.

"Youn Hee," I said when Simon went off to the bath she had gotten ready for him, "would you teach me how to do that neat airplane you made for Simon?"

"Sure," she said. "Come to our room and I teach you."

"I thought origami was Japanese," I said as we sat across from each other at the old dining room table Mom had given us to use as a double desk.

"Korean word not *origami*," she said, "but we fold, too. See?" She showed me step-by-step how to do airplanes, and I watched and tried to imitate her. Youn Hee had learned to do dozens of things she didn't know how to do when she came here—just by watching us and doing it the way we did it. But I couldn't seem to learn that way. I was so sloppy at paper-folding that Youn Hee puffed out her lips at the plane I produced. She didn't put me down about it though.

Suddenly we both got the same idea and shot our planes into the air. They crossed paths before one landed on my bed and the other on the floor.

"Mine is one on the floor," Youn Hee said slowly and with care. Recently she'd been trying to put the little connecting words into her sentences. "Because I am Korean, and we like to sleep on floor—the floor."

"Oh," I said. "Yeah." I remembered that first night her bed came. I'd awakened when she'd rolled off and bumped on the floor. She'd been embarrassed. She slept fine on the bed now.

We were getting along so well that I asked her to tell me about her friend in the orphanage. I'd found out all the letters she wrote were going to one person.

"Hee Sook misses me," Youn Hee said. "The head, the—like a principal of the orphanage?"

"Yes."

"She do not like Hee Sook. She said Hee Sook is stupid and slow, but Hee Sook cannot help it. So when she wants something, I get it for her. I ask. The head give it me because she like me."

"So then how come Hee Sook doesn't answer your letters?"

"She can't write good. Hee Sook—" Youn Hee shrugged and scrunched her cheeks up as if she were pained. "She not a good student, but she is good—a good girl."

Like me, I thought. Or anyway, I used to think I was good before Youn Hee came and I turned out to have so many faults. "Maybe we should send Hee Sook some presents," I said.

"Presents?"

"Yes, little things she would like. We could go to the mall. I have some allowance left." I meant after having bought Mom, Simon, and my father Christmas presents. I hadn't thought of anything for Youn Hee yet.

Youn Hee clapped her hands. "Me, too. I have allowance. Oh, that is good idea, Caitlin. We do that. Ask Mommy when."

Mom was so pleased that we wanted to do something together that she took us to the mall the next night even though she hates going shopping during the Christmas crush. To make things easy for us, she went off with Simon, who was now fully recovered and needed new sneakers. He always needs new sneakers.

Youn Hee and I stopped to see the animated display of Santa and his elves making toys in the middle of the mall. Then we started shopping at the discount drugstore, which was decorated with candy canes and gold tinsel. It was a good choice. Youn Hee got her friend pink scented soap and some bright-colored barrettes. That used up her allowance. I got Hee Sook Magic Markers, a drawing pad, and a picture frame that was a terrific markdown.

"We can put one of the photographs Mom took of you in it. I bet Hee Sook would like that," I told Youn Hee.

"Yes, yes, thank you, Caitlin," Youn Hee said. She clapped her hands with delight and I was tickled.

We passed a toy store with some Barbie dolls in the window. I gave away my last Barbie years ago, but Youn Hee seemed fascinated. "I wish we didn't use up all the money," she said shyly.

"Why, would Hee Sook like a doll?"

"I don't know. Maybe. She is old. Older than me. But—"

Her face was so wistful that I asked, "Youn Hee, would you like a Barbie doll?"

"I never had one," she admitted.

"And I never got you a welcome present," I said.

"You don't have to."

"But I want to." Especially now that we were getting along better. I looked at the price. The money I'd set aside for Youn Hee's Christmas present wouldn't cover it. I grabbed Youn Hee's hand and went running to find Mom. She was still in the sneaker store.

Breathlessly I explained that I needed to buy something very important and would she give me an advance on January's allowance. Without asking questions, Mom handed me the money I needed, and I raced Youn Hee back to the store as if it might be out of Barbie dolls unless we hurried. She picked one with a pink net, rhinestone-trimmed ball gown.

When I'd paid for the doll and Youn Hee had it in her hands, her smile could have lit up the mall. I managed to buy a surprise Christmas present for her while she was busy admiring her Barbie. I felt great that she was so happy and I had my shopping all done.

"So, Youn Hee," I said. "What are you going to name her?"

"Barbie," she said.

"Yeah, your Barbie doll. What are you going to name her?"

"Her name is Barbie," Youn Hee said it as if I were a dimwit.

"You know," I said. "*You* could have an American name, too. I was thinking you look sort of like an Amy."

"My name is Youn Hee."

"But an American name—"

"I am Korean. My name is mine." Youn Hee's eyes froze me out.

Trailing Mom, Youn Hee, and Simon through the food court en route to the parking lot, I saw Audrey and Bud and Denise sitting at a table. "Hey, guys," I yelled. "What are you doing here?"

"Buying Christmas presents," Audrey said.

Bud unloaded shopping bags from a chair to make room for me, and I sat down deciding Mom, Youn Hee, and Simon could wait in the car for me for a minute. "How come you didn't invite me to go shopping with you?" I asked.

"We did," Denise said, "but you were taking care of your sick brother, remember?"

"Oh yeah." I did remember. Denise had asked me at lunch, before I knew when Simon was going back to school. "Did you have fun?" I asked, sorry I hadn't been with them.

"Nah," Bud said, "Audrey and I had a big fight over this frog in the nature store, and we broke its foot off and had to pay for it."

"I'm going to give it to my brother," Audrey said. "He won't notice it's been glued."

"We're going to have a sleep-over at my house during Christmas week," Denise said. "Can you come, Caitlin or . . . ?"

"Sure," I said promptly, and didn't ask if I could bring Youn Hee. I wanted to, but I was afraid my friends might be sick of having to include her any time they wanted me.

Denise must have read my mind though because she said, "You can bring Youn Hee if she wants to come, Caitlin."

"Thanks," I said. "I'll ask her." I was so grateful they hadn't shut me out of the group that I gave them each a quick hug before I ran for the car and my waiting family.

That night Youn Hee and I fought over who was going to help Simon brush his teeth. And the next day, when I asked her if she wanted to go shares in the present I'd gotten for Mom, she said, "I have my own present for Mommy."

I got the message all right. Youn Hee still meant to return to Korea in the spring, with or without Simon.

Chapter Eleven

Youn Hee and I were having such fun wrapping our Christmas presents for her friend Hee Sook that I got the idea of including some sweaters I'd outgrown and barely worn. Youn Hee immediately added one of her two pairs of jeans to the pile of stuff we were wrapping to send. "One pair is enough for me," she said. She was just deciding she could send one of everything she had two of when Mom came into our room. She called a halt to our giving spree as soon as we told her what we were doing.

"Youn Hee, you need those clothes," Mom said. "If you give them away, I'll just have to replace them, and that will wreck our budget."

"Budget?" Youn Hee asked.

Mom explained that part of her salary was for the house and part of it for food and part for clothes and part for insurance with a little left over for emergencies, but not much.

"You're not rich?" Youn Hee sounded so amazed that Mom and I had to laugh.

"Did you think we were, Youn Hee?"

"Oh yes! You have big house and so much nice furniture and clothes and car and washer machines."

"Well, but we're not rich, Youn Hee, not even close," Mom said. "I earn enough to buy what we need if we're careful, but if we spend too much, I'll go into debt, and then I wouldn't sleep nights."

"But Simon has so many toys."

Mom had to agree, but she explained, "You see, my husband left us right after Simon came, and that upset Simon very much. So I got in the habit of giving him toys to make him happy." Mom shrugged. "He doesn't get so many new toys now."

Youn Hee wasn't finished though. She said, "But when we don't eat up our dinner, you throw it away."

"Yes, it's too bad. If Caitlin weren't so allergic to fur, we'd have an animal we could feed leftovers to," Mom said.

"But, you use paper and paper and paper," Youn Hee protested. "We could save and use backs, or cut up small. We could dry bottoms of pots with cloth not paper towel." She went on and on—it was like she'd stuffed everything that bothered her into some closet in her mind that had now burst open.

"We do waste a lot, Youn Hee," Mom admitted, "but we're still not rich. Compared to other Americans anyway. Maybe we should be more careful."

"Yes, *more careful*," Youn Hee said. Her eyes fixed on Simon who was nose-to-nose with the TV. "Not fill the bathtub for just one small boy."

"He needs enough water to float his boats," I offered in Simon's defense.

"And turn off shower between soap and rinse. That save water." Youn Hee was frowning my way as she said that. I do enjoy letting the hot water pour over me, it's true.

"You keep an eye on us, Youn Hee," Mom said. "We *should* become more conservation-minded, for the sake of the environment as well."

"Yes, I watch," Youn Hee said with determination.

"Oh no!" I moaned. Somehow we'd gone from not being rich to a crusade for saving resources. Worse, we had a kitten-faced police person in charge who could watch day and night to ensure my cooperation.

Sure enough, Youn Hee caught me letting the water run that evening while I was brushing my teeth. "Turn it off until you rinse," she ordered. I was tempted to tell her she was Simon's Noo na, not mine, but I meekly shut off the faucet instead.

The big package Mom mailed off to Korea a couple of days later included a bunch of toys Simon said he didn't want anymore. Youn Hee wrote a note in Korean to Hee Sook asking her to give the toys to any younger kids who'd like them. I wished I could see Hee Sook's face when she got the package. "I hope she'll write us about it soon," I said.

"Don't hold your breath," Mom warned me. "It could take a month or more for the package to get to her."

With one more day to go until Christmas Eve, Mom heard about a Korean fair being held at a church in Albany and hustled us off to it.

As soon as we entered the church basement where the fair was being held, Youn Hee took a deep breath and said happily, "*Kim chee.*"

"Who?" I asked.

"*Kim chee.* It's delicious."

We got in line at the food table. Youn Hee fizzed with excitement, telling us what each dish was and encouraging us to try her favorites. She had all the Korean ladies who were serving food in their traditional dresses giggling as they watched us.

We sat down at a table together and began sampling the dishes on our trays. I wasn't too wild about the *kim chee.* It was cabbage, my least favorite vegetable, and so peppery I gulped half my glass of water after one bite. The best food as far as I was concerned was a kind of dumpling called *mahn-doo.*

"Korean food is good, isn't it, Si Won?" Youn Hee asked him. She'd been calling him Simon for a while, but this was Korean night I guessed.

"I like McDonald's better," Simon said.

Youn Hee's smile dipped at the corners, but she perked up when Mom offered to give us each five dollars to spend at the gift counter. I picked a miniature doll in Korean dress that looked just like Youn Hee. She clapped her hands in delight when she found a Korean music tape. "The fan dance. I do it for you," she told Mom. Simon took the longest to settle on something because he wanted so many things, mostly too expensive. He ended up with a balsa-wood plane.

Christmas Eve we decorated a small live evergreen. My dream of a replacement for the shabby old fake tree had been something beautiful and tall and freshly cut, but I'd had to admit that it would have been a shame to dump it at the curb after New Year's to be carted off by the garbage truck. The live evergreen was more conservation-minded.

"I should make Youn Hee dig the hole for this," Mom grumbled as I helped her lug in the tree and set it up on plastic on our living-room rug. What made it so heavy was the huge ball of burlap-wrapped dirt around its roots.

"Can't we wait until spring to plant it if we keep it watered?" I asked.

"Good idea," Mom said. "Anyway, it's worth a try." She shoved the tree upright, put her hand on the small of her back, and added, "And all three of you can dig the hole without my help."

"You can't get out of it, Mom. You're the one who thought it was so great that Youn Hee doesn't like to waste stuff."

Mom's only response was a grunt.

We took turns hanging the ornaments. Youn Hee had made two pretty gold foil cranes that she hung, and I got to put the dainty angel on the top. Simon liked the nutcracker figures best, so he hung those.

Christmas morning when we got up, Simon had already opened all his presents and was playing with his space station. Mom scolded him for cheating us out of the pleasure of watching him open his gifts. "We wanted to see how much you like them, Simon," Mom said.

"I like them," he assured her.

"Simon, you bad boy," Youn Hee said. "You must not think only of yourself. You must do what pleases your mommy."

"Want me to wrap them up and open them again?" Simon asked. It would have been quite a trick. He'd carpeted the floor in ripped-up Christmas wrap.

"Just say thank you, and you can watch the rest of us open our gifts," I said. I was hoping the large square box had a new soccer ball for me. Sure enough it did, and I whooped and tossed the ball in the air and bounced it around the room, kissing Mom to thank her along the way.

Youn Hee wasn't in a hurry to open her gifts.

"First I have one for you, Mommy," she said, and dashed upstairs for it.

While we were waiting, Mom went in to start the pancakes we always had for breakfast on Christmas morning. Dad used to make them for Mom and me. It's funny I remember that because I don't remember much we did together when he lived with us. His pancakes came out perfectly round I remember. Mom's never did, but they tasted just as good.

Youn Hee finally came down in the Korean dress she'd brought on the plane with her. She gave me her Korean music tape to put in the tape deck, and she got Mom and Simon to sit on the couch.

I don't know what the fan dance is supposed to look like, but the one Youn Hee did was really pretty. Her eyes teased us above the fan, and her hands were little birds playing with each other as the fan opened and closed its tail and swooped and rose and stretched in elegant loops around her head. Even the strange twangy sound of the music seemed pretty the way she moved to it.

We applauded when she finished, Simon loudest of all. Then Youn Hee bowed to Mom and presented the fan to her. "Thank you for all you have done for my brother and me. This is my fan that I brought from Korea. It is for you," she said.

Mom got all teary-eyed. "I couldn't take your fan, Youn Hee. That wouldn't be right. Besides I can't dance with it the way you can."

"But I want you to have it," Youn Hee assured her.

Mom said, "I know! I'll hang it on the wall here in the living room so when you want to use it, you can just take it down. How's that?"

Youn Hee smiled. "If I need to use it, I will ask may I because it is yours now."

Mom thanked her for it and said it was a lovely gift. I thought it was lovely, too. My gift to Mom was just a pair of pink velour stretchy slippers. But Simon liked the friction race car I gave him and Youn Hee liked the new Barbie doll outfit I'd bought her, so I felt pretty good. Oh yeah, and I liked the book from Youn Hee—it was a mystery—and the whistle from Simon. Besides the soccer ball, Mom had gotten me a sweater. She'd gotten one for Youn Hee, too, plus a book.

The phone rang and Mom jumped. "Want to answer that, Caitlin?" she asked.

I ran for it, expecting it to be my father, but it was just Uncle Derek. "Mom, Uncle Derek wants to know when we're coming."

She took the phone from me.

I guess my disappointment must have been obvious because Youn Hee asked me, "Who did you think it was?"

"My father," I said. "Sometimes he calls to wish us a Merry Christmas, but mostly he forgets."

"Why don't you call him?"

I snorted. "Once Mom called him and put me on the phone, but Dad and his wife were catching a plane for Barbados, so he couldn't talk to me. . . . I don't really have much to say to him anyway. Usually he remembers to send Simon and me a check and I thank him for that." I shrugged. "I don't know why it bothers me so much when Dad forgets to call. I guess it's something about Christmas that makes me want a father."

"You could write him," Youn Hee said.

"Yeah, and he could write me. If he doesn't care that I'm his daughter, why should I care?"

"Because he's your father." Youn Hee put so much feeling in the word *father* that I could see it waving in the breeze like a flag. I wasn't saluting though.

"So who needs a father?" I argued. "Mom's good enough for two parents."

"Yes," Youn Hee said. "But you *have* two parents, and that's lucky, Caitlin. Really, you are very lucky."

"I know," I said. I wished she'd leave me alone. It just bothered me when Dad forgot to call, and she was making it worse.

As we drove to Uncle Derek's house later that afternoon, I was cheerful enough again to think how much fun it was to have both a brother and a sister to share Christmas with this year. A big family is more festive.

I hoped eating dinner with Uncle Derek wasn't going to tarnish the tinsel. Last year they had come to our house—Uncle Derek, who was Mom's younger brother, and his second wife, Doris. She was rich and a lot older than him. They had come with great presents for us, but my uncle had drunk too much and gotten into an argument with my mom. Mom had said we'd never spend another Christmas with her brother, but then a few days later he'd called to apologize. Mom had said after all he was the only family she had. So they'd made up, and here we were going to their house for this Christmas. Mom thought going to them might work out better. I sure hoped so.

"Don't worry about whatever Uncle Derek says to you, Youn Hee," I warned her in the car. "Just pretend you don't understand if you don't like it."

"Why? What does he say?"

"Oh, stupid things sometimes. He may be all right. Don't worry."

When we got to Uncle Derek's house, I was sorry I'd said anything because Youn Hee acted too shy and quiet through the introductions. Immediately afterward, we kids were sent off to watch the huge TV that's built into a wall of the den. Aunt Doris had rented a Disney movie for us, and it was almost like seeing it in the movie house. The movie turned out to be too young for me though, so I joined Mom and Aunt Doris in the kitchen. Aunt Doris was basting the turkey.

Uncle Derek came into the kitchen, too. "Make you a drink?" he asked Mom.

"No thanks, Derek. I'll have some wine with dinner if you're serving any."

"Have some now." He opened a bottle and poured her a glassful even though she'd said she'd rather wait.

I helped Aunt Doris put little hors d'oeuvres from the freezer onto a platter to put in the microwave.

"So how are you managing with three kids?" Uncle Derek asked Mom.

"Fine. They're no problem, anyway not for me. Caitlin's the one to ask."

"Yeah," he said. "So, Caitlin, how do you like having another Korean kid in the family?"

"Fine," I said.

"You get along with the new one OK?"

"Sure."

"Caitlin would get along with anybody," Aunt Doris said.

"So when are you going to bring the rest of the orphanage over?" Uncle Derek asked Mom.

"Three kids are enough for me," she said.

"Three kids and no husband. Yeah, that should keep you busy," he said.

"Mom likes kids," I said.

"She sure must, any kind, even brown and yellow," he said.

"How is your jewelry-making going, Doris?" Mom asked. No question she was trying to change the subject.

"Wonderful. I was in a craft show last week with my partner. We almost sold out."

"That's great." Mom turned her back on her brother and kept pumping out questions about the beads Aunt Doris used in making her fancy necklaces.

At dinner Uncle Derek asked Youn Hee, "You need a pair of chopsticks to eat with?"

"No, thank you."

"I've got a pair. I saved them from a Chink

restaurant. Your people eat with chopsticks, too, don't they?"

"Yes," Youn Hee said.

"You're a cute little thing," he said, "but you don't smile much, do you? Let's see you smile."

Youn Hee tried to oblige.

"Yeah," he said. "Your eyes disappear when you smile just like your brother's do."

"Yours disappear, too, Derek, after you've tossed down a few," Mom said, "like about now."

"Oh, please don't start in, you two," Doris said. "I worked hard on this dinner. Let's eat it, shall we?"

I held my breath. Mom was staring at her brother waiting to see what he'd say next. He swallowed a few times and wiped his mouth with his napkin. "I was just joking with the kid," he said. "Can't you take a little joke?"

In the backseat of the car on the way home, Youn Hee whispered to me, "I don't like your uncle."

"I don't like him much either," I told her quietly. "He's OK sometimes though.

Like at ball games. He likes ball games."

"Nobody around here is Korean," Youn Hee said sadly.

"What do you mean?" I asked her. "What about at that fair we went to? And there's Korean people who live near us."

"Not in our school."

"Sure there are. There's a boy in eighth grade and a pair of twins I've seen around."

"They're not Korean."

"Oh, well, anyway they're Asian."

"Korean is just as good as anybody here, better maybe."

"Right," I said.

"Simon, Si Won, doesn't know any Korean words."

"You've taught him some, haven't you?"

"He couldn't even play *yout*. He didn't know what to call me when I came. He thinks his skin is wrong and his eyes. But they are right—in Korea." I saw the tears in her eyes before she turned away.

"Youn Hee, I thought you were beginning to like it here. I thought we were beginning to become sisters."

"We can't be sisters, Caitlin. I'm Korean and you're not."

"But Youn Hee . . ."

"And Si Won's Korean even if he doesn't want to be." She was looking out the window, and I didn't know what to say. Besides, I didn't want her to see that she had me crying now, too.

Chapter Twelve

Denise's sleep-over was a big success. We stayed up until three A.M. teasing each other and giggling. Even Youn Hee giggled. The rest of the week was quiet. Then came New Year's Day.

Mom's department always gave a New Year's Day party for everybody who worked there and their families. Simon loved it, and he'd been a big hit last year until he'd tipped over the punch bowl trying to get himself a refill. Mom told Youn Hee how much her office staff was looking forward to meeting her this year. "You can wear the red velvet party dress you wore to Uncle Derek's house for Christmas," Mom said.

"I wear my Korean dress," Youn Hee said.

"Fine," Mom said. "You look lovely in that, too, Youn Hee. And would you like to perform the fan dance? That would be a treat for everybody."

"No!" Youn Hee shouted.

Mom backed off immediately. "I just thought you do it so well," she said, "but of course, if you're shy in front of strangers?" She made it a question, but Youn Hee didn't explain.

I put on my party dress an hour before we were supposed to leave and admired myself in the long mirror in Mom's room. It's the only dress I ever liked on me. It has this big, white, open-necked collar and it's a marbly, dark-colored velvet gathered to make it fuller around the hips. I suppose it sounds terrible, but really, considering I'm built like a long, straight carrot, it looks good.

Simon came in wearing his best pants, with his shirt hanging out below his red vest. I tucked his shirt in and kissed him because he looked so cute.

"Hey," he said. "Stop that. Want me to punch you?"

"You can't. I'm all dressed up."

That made enough sense to calm Simon down. He even said, "You look nice, Caitlin."

We went downstairs to be admired by Mom, and then we three waited for Youn

Hee. She came down in her red-and-yellow Korean dress with the ribbon at the neck. The dress didn't look so great because Youn Hee's arms and legs stuck out of it too much. Besides, her eyes were glazed as if she'd been crying.

"You look very pretty, Youn Hee," Mom said anyway.

Youn Hee folded her lips in. "It doesn't fit," she said in a very small voice.

"Well, it's gotten a bit small on you maybe. Want to change to your other dress?"

"No."

"OK, then let's go." Mom never was one to worry much about how things look.

Youn Hee hesitated. "I stay home," she said finally.

"Youn Hee!" Mom said in a tone of voice that made Youn Hee hang her head and give in without another word.

Mom handed us our coats and led the way to the car.

Youn Hee was quiet in the backseat, and I didn't have anything to say. Simon did all the talking. He told us the whole plot of the movie he'd seen on TV that afternoon, every gory, boring detail. None of us seemed to be listening, but nobody stopped him either. I was remembering how hard it had been for me to get used to living with a two-year-old when Simon came. He kept invading my room and messing up everything, and I guess I inherited some genes from my father all right because I like things neat. I don't remember how long it took me to start loving Simon. All I know is now I wouldn't change him for any other little brother in the world. Was it possible I'd ever feel that way about Youn Hee? It didn't seem likely. But I did feel sorry for her about outgrowing her Korean dress. It was one of the few treasures from Korea that she hadn't given away.

Mom's office building is a huge old Victorian house with a sign out front saying it's the Child Care and Development Agency. The staff had cleared out the desks from the middle of the floor in the main room and put in a table with refreshments. In front of the Christmas tree, somebody dressed up like a snowman was leading all the kids in games.

"Wait until someone pours you your punch, Simon," Mom reminded him.

"I'm a big boy now," he said, throwing out his chest. She raised an eyebrow at him and said his name warningly, and he grumbled under his breath.

The adults mostly sat on folding chairs around the walls, talking to each other and eating the sandwiches, cookies, and punch while they bounced babies on their knees and kept an eye on their older kids. Mom introduced us to people. Of course, everyone said nice things about how we looked and how big our family had grown, and teased Mom about her getting another child without having to carry it around for nine months and give birth to it. I got asked how I felt about getting a full-grown sister.

"Fine," I said. I mean, what are you supposed to say when someone you don't know asks you a question that personal? Youn Hee got through it by being polite and saying very little.

Someone offered us a dish of nuts. I took a handful, and Youn Hee took one and said thank you. The lady laughed at her. "Just one?" she teased. "Are you on a diet, honey?"

That embarrassed Youn Hee so much she dropped her eyes and refused to take any more nuts even though they're her favorite snack. She left me and found a chair as far away from people as she could get. I shrugged and took Simon off to join in the games.

They were baby games because most of the kids were preschoolers, but it was something to do and Simon enjoyed himself. He puts a lot of energy into stomping on balloons and playing musical chairs and Simon says, which he thinks was named for him. Finally the snowman made us take a number and handed out gifts. Youn Hee wouldn't get up, although I waved her over, so I asked if I could have an extra gift for my sister. What I got was the kind of game where you roll little beads into holes. Simon got a small xylophone, which he immediately started banging. I don't know what Youn Hee got because she wouldn't unwrap her gift. She just sat there holding it.

"What's the matter?" I asked her.

"Nothing." She looked miserable and pale. I didn't know if it was an inside hurt or if her shoes were pinching her.

"We'll be going home soon. These parties never last long," I told her, and left her sitting it out until Mom told us to get our coats.

Usually, Mom asks us how we enjoyed ourselves when we're on the way home from something, but she knew better than to ask us that night. She'd seen Youn Hee's face. Simon volunteered that he'd had fun, but when he fell asleep in the front seat, the car got so quiet I noticed the engine's hum and heard other cars swishing past us on the road. Mom glanced over her shoulder at Youn Hee and raised an eyebrow at me. I shrugged. I didn't have a clue to what was wrong except maybe that she'd outgrown her Korean dress. Frankly, I was getting tired of Youn Hee not enjoying fun things. It made them less fun for me. Most of all, I didn't like the way she kept taking over as Simon's sister, as if she were the real one and I was fake. I couldn't help thinking it would have been better for us all if we'd left her in that orphanage in Korea.

Chapter Thirteen

The night after the office party, Mom dropped the three of us off at the library while she went to do the food shopping. Simon went straight to the puzzles on the kiddie tables next to the picture book shelves, and Youn Hee and I cruised the fiction shelves looking for books we hadn't read.

"Did you get to go to the library much when you lived in Korea, Youn Hee?" I asked. I knew she loved books because after the first day when she'd only picked one book and seemed surprised they let her take it out, she always carried home a double arm-load. I think she read them all, too. At least, she always had her nose in a book when I saw her.

"We don't have libraries in Korea," Youn Hee said. "Only in the schools. Well, they do have libraries, but not for kids, I think."

"Really? So that's something good about here."

She wouldn't even agree to that. Instead she said, "In Korea there are many mountains."

"We have mountains in New York and lots in the rest of the country. The Adirondacks are only about an hour away. Want to ask Mom to take us for a drive so we can show them to you?"

Youn Hee considered while she took another of the Laura Ingalls Wilder books she liked from the shelf. "In Korea shopping is nicer," she said.

"Really? You mean the malls are fancier?"

"No. No malls. The shops are all"—she set her books down on a table so she could show me with her hands—"little and close together so it's noisy and lots of tables on the sidewalk. You talk to people more and it's more . . ." She shrugged.

"Friendly?"

"Yes, friendly. And you can walk to the stores. Here you have to go in a car everywhere."

"Not always. By next summer we'll

probably be allowed to ride bikes to the mall." I stopped. What did she care? She wasn't planning to be here next summer. Before she could remind me of that, I asked, "Did you go shopping a lot when you were at the orphanage?"

She nodded enthusiastically. "Yes, sometimes they took me to help carry packages. The head lady liked me, and she let me help."

"What else was good about the orphanage?" I asked glumly. No question Youn Hee was building up a case for why she wanted to go back after the six months' probation period was up.

"Nothing good about it," Youn Hee said cheerfully. "We didn't have much food and no toys. And school had such big classes with twice as much kids as here and lots and lots and lots of homework. Always homework and chores until you go to bed. No time to play. We had to clean our classrooms ourselves. My friend and I, we pushed the broom together up and down between rows of desks. That was fun."

"Cleaning the room was fun?"

"Yes, together. And in Korea kids do more

singing and dancing. We are always singing songs while we work."

"We sing songs at Christmas here."

"Yes, but not so much the rest of the year like in Korea. And we have New Year's party when the families get together and you play *yout* and eat all kinds of good things like rice cakes. And on New Year's Day children bow to parents in the morning and wish them health and happiness, and the parents give children money and good wishes and children wear Korean dress. Not like office party you have here."

"But who did you bow to in the orphanage?"

"We had a party and we bowed to the head lady and I wore my dress. Yes . . . And there is lunar New Year. That is another time by a different calendar from here, and everybody gets a year older then." She frowned in confusion and added, "Or maybe on January first new year, you get a year older."

"Then you don't have birthdays?"

"Yes, but you don't get a year older. On your birthday you get served first. The rest of the year the father or the head lady gets served first. But on your birthday, you get served first and everyone says Happy Birthday, and you get to start eating first. It's nice."

It didn't sound like a big deal to me, but I could see by the way she was sparkling that she thought it was. "We could do that here," I said.

"But you don't have the right food. In Korea for your birthday you get seaweed soup with beef and a rice cake. *Miyuk-gook* is seaweed soup. They don't have it here."

"I bet we could get the right stuff for it at that Oriental market near the mall, Youn Hee. Want to ask Mom if we can make seaweed soup? When's your birthday?"

"Not till May. Anyway, you don't like *kim chee*."

"Well, I'm not Korean."

"No, you're not."

I sighed and asked her, because I really wanted to know, "Why do you miss it so much, Youn Hee? I mean, is it the people you miss or just the food and that kind of thing?"

She picked up her load of books and rested her chin on top of the stack as she thought.

"I miss being where I know how to be. In Korea I am Korean. Here, I can*not* be Korean. But I'm not American, and I don't look right. And I don't know the right way how to do things here." Her voice was so sad it made me want to cry.

"You haven't been here very long. You'll get used to it, Youn Hee."

"No. Simon can be American, but I cannot be."

And she didn't want to be. I could see that.

We collected Simon and took our books to the sign-out counter. I didn't say it to Youn Hee, but I wondered if she might become American anyway, even if she didn't want to—if she stayed long enough. After all, everyone in this country originally came from somewhere else. Except the Indians were already here. But even some of them migrated across from Asia when the continents were connected thousands of years ago—tens of thousands, I guess. I wondered if it would take Youn Hee tens of thousands of years to feel at home in the good old U.S.A. I wished there were more Korean girls her age in our school. Being the only one in our class made it tough. I imagined myself being adopted by a Korean family and having to go to school where everybody had straight black hair and eyelids with a fold, and I looked too different to blend in. Would I be as unhappy then as Youn Hee? Somehow I expected I'd be more like Simon and begin to see myself as Korean even if my hair and skin and eyes were different. . . . But maybe not.

I didn't know if Youn Hee thought I was upset with her for the things she'd said about Korea, or what, but suddenly when we were in the backseat of the car and Simon was up front listening to a folktale on the tape deck, she started to talk to me again.

"Caitlin?"

"What?"

"First thing when I come to your house you know what I thought?"

"What?"

"I thought, everything is so nice. The house is so big with so much nice furniture and so many rooms. And Simon has so so much. I thought, he doesn't want a Korean sister. He has a better American one that plays ball with him. And I thought, they will think I am stupid because I cannot speak their language right and I don't know how to do things. I didn't know about the dishwasher or the wall oven. We didn't have that in the orphanage. We had top of stove cooking and people do the dishes. No VCR, no lots of things like answering machines and lawns. We don't have lawns in Korea— anyway not big grass spaces, just little flowers to make a garden sometimes. But not at the orphanage. No place to play outside, and too crowded in the park . . . Caitlin?"

"What?"

She leaned toward me and confessed earnestly, "I hated the picnics in Korea that come in the spring and fall. They have them in special places, like an old palace or famous garden. It is so crowded, and parents bring lots of food for their children. And orphan children don't have so much food and no parents. I hated that. . . . And New Year's. I hated not having parents to bow to then."

"I'm sorry, Youn Hee."

"Tell me true, Caitlin," Youn Hee said suddenly. "Was it because Simon was bad that your father left?"

"Simon? Oh no, Youn Hee," I said. "I

mean, my father's not that crazy about kids, and Simon was a wild two-year-old, but it was me, not Simon, who Dad couldn't take. Like he'd try to help me with schoolwork and he'd get frustrated and call me stupid. I just wasn't the little girl doll he'd expected. My voice was too loud and I jumped and ran around and banged into things instead of crayoning in coloring books. Mom liked me anyway, but my father didn't."

"You could be good," Youn Hee said, "if you wanted. You are good now, sometimes. True?"

"True," I said, and smiled.

"If I had a father, I would try to please him," Youn Hee said.

"You have a mother and a brother and me," I said.

Youn Hee shook her head in her stubborn way. "Simon is all I have, and I must take care of him. See he grows up good."

"Was it because of Simon? Was that why you were mad at me that first night when we picked you up at the train station?" I asked her.

"Simon? No. I got mad because you called me wrong. You said *uhn nee* to me, and that means older sister, and I am not your old sister." She shrugged. "But also Simon. He was not like I remembered, and he didn't know me."

"He was only two when you got separated, Youn Hee."

"I know, but still it scared me that he didn't know me."

We were quiet for a long time. Suddenly Youn Hee said, "I wish Hee Sook would write."

"Maybe she didn't get the presents yet. The mail sometimes takes forever, and Korea's very far away."

"Yes, far," Youn Hee agreed in a voice thin as wind.

"Youn Hee," I said. "I'm sorry it's hard for you here, even though I try—Mom and I both try—to make it easy. But I wish you'd stay. I wish you'd try to be my sister. Please."

"Caitlin," she said looking me square in the eyes. "I know you try, but I cannot be your sister because of Simon."

"What do you mean?"

"I can't explain it. I'm sorry," she said. She turned away from me then to put an end to the discussion.

Well, I'd begged her. I'd said *please*. What

else could I do? Nothing, I told myself. She'd made up her mind. I was going to miss her when she left. Even though she wasn't much fun sometimes, even though she wanted to take my brother away from me—I was going to miss her.

Chapter Fourteen

We got our first snow day the second week in January. I couldn't believe it when I woke up because I had given up hope, but now every branch of every tree in sight had arm-loads of snow weighing it down. The garbage pail out at the curb for pick-up had a top hat of snow, and the only way I could tell where the street was was from the truck tracks zippering down it.

"No school!" I shouted, and rolled Youn Hee out of her bed.

"What?" She blinked at me as if I were nuts.

"We're going to have a snow day. Look outside. See it out there? They'll never get the buses through *that*. I'm going downstairs to hear the school-closing announcements." I used the banister as a safety line to rappel down the stairs.

Simon was already up. He was sitting barefooted on the kitchen floor in his pajamas in front of the wide-open sliding-glass door. That way he could sit inside and play with the snow outside on the back deck. "Look, I'm making snowballs," he said, holding one up for me to see.

"You're going to make us freeze to death, Simon." I dragged him back and shut the door. He felt like an ice cube and his hands were a chilly red. "We'll go out and play in it later," I promised him. "But first we eat breakfast."

Youn Hee helped me cook hot oatmeal. One of the things I like about her is the way she pitches in on any chore without being asked. Not only that, she cleans the bathroom after us, which is the job I hate most. Usually I leave it for Mom or the cleaning person, but there hasn't been any caked toothpaste in the sinks since Youn Hee came.

Mom came down dressed for work. "Why do you have that radio on so loud?" she asked me.

"So we don't miss anything," I said.

Just then they began announcing school

closings. "Yes!" I shouted in triumph when they read our school district's name.

"Yes!" Simon echoed me, shooting his fist in the air.

"I was going to help Mrs. Howe in the library today," Youn Hee murmured as if it disappointed her to have to stay home.

"You can help her tomorrow," I said.

"No, tomorrow is gym."

"Youn Hee, we're going to have FUN. We'll build a humongous snowman. We'll have a snowball fight. We'll—we'll go sledding over on the golf course."

She eyed me as if I were speaking a foreign language. Well, of course, it *was* for her, but not so much anymore. She'd really learned English fast.

"I'm going to try to drive to work," Mom said. "You guys be careful. I'll let Hettie know she's on call today, and if you need me, you know the number at the office." She made Youn Hee and Simon recite it before she left. "Be sure you check in with Hettie so she knows where to find you."

"We know, Mom. Don't worry," I said.

"Do you get snow in Korea, Youn Hee?" I asked her while we were putting on the insulated underwear Mom had bought us for outdoor play.

"Oh yes, it snows."

"Well, what do you do outside when it snows?"

"I don't go out then," she said.

I stopped in midsock pull. "You *don't*? You're kidding. Why not?"

She rolled her lip out and frowned at me as if the question stumped her.

"Never mind," I said. "Today you'll see what you've been missing. Come on."

We zipped up Simon's ski parka and talked him into a hat and scarf and gloves, and with me on the big shovel and Youn Hee on Simon's toy shovel and Simon supervising, we cleared the walk and the steps to the house fast. The snowplow guy Mom hires was supposed to take care of the driveway before she got home from work.

Next we built a snowman. We gave him crescent moon eyes cut from a plastic plant container. He wore my raggedy knitted hat from last year, and we finished him off with a red potato nose and a red plastic bottle-top mouth. He was so tall, I had to hoist Simon up to put the hat on.

A snowball hit me in the head as I was holding Simon up. A bunch of little kids from the neighborhood, including two of Hettie's grandchildren, were hopping around like popcorn behind the bushes across the street.

"Want to have a war?" one yelled.

"No fair," I said. "There's lots of you and only three of us." Not to mention that I didn't expect Youn Hee to be much help in a war. She was though. As soon as the missiles started flying at us, we took cover behind our forsythia bush hedge, and she went to work manufacturing snowballs. Simon was too excited to pack balls right. Like a manic snowblower, he kept throwing handfuls of snow that went nowhere.

"Hey, little samurai," I told him. "You've got to *make* your ammunition before you can shoot with it."

"I make balls, you throw," Youn Hee said. She was a one-woman snowball factory, but we were getting hit by so many so often we couldn't see to throw.

"Charge, Simon," I yelled, and I went leaping across the street right into the arms of the enemy. Simon screeched a war cry and followed on my heels. When we got tired

155

of rolling around in the snow with the gang we'd attacked, I looked around for Youn Hee and couldn't find her. Coward, I thought. She'd run inside and left us to our fate. But then I saw her clomping toward us from the garage with the broom.

"Hey, no fair!" the first kid she whacked with the broom said. After the second one got hit, they all took off.

I lay back in the snow laughing so hard I couldn't get up. When I finally did, I had to tell her: "Youn Hee, this was a play war. Only snowballs, no sticks allowed."

She glared at me. "Crazy girl!" she said in disgust. Then she stomped back across the street to put the broom away.

"What's she so mad about?" Simon asked me.

"I don't know. She's your sister."

"Yours, too," he shot back.

But I knew better. I began wondering which of us Simon would choose when Youn Hee left—and then I stopped. Why ruin the day worrying? "Let's go eat lunch," I said. "This afternoon the snow should be great for sledding on the golf course. Want to go?"

"*OK!*" Simon agreed with enthusiasm.

He had two sandwiches for lunch. I had two and a half. Being outdoors in winter always doubles my appetite. Youn Hee had her usual bite-size sandwich and a banana.

She didn't want to go sledding with us. "I stay home and read my book," she said, nodding happily at the idea.

"Oh, come on, Youn Hee. This may be the only good snow we get all year. Sledding's fun."

She shook her head. It was only when Simon wheedled her to come along that she reluctantly got back into her outside clothes and joined us.

"But no fighting," she said.

"Absatively not," I said, and to mock her a little, I added, "We don't want you beating anybody up with brooms again."

That made her so angry at me that I had to apologize twice before we could persuade her not to stay home after all. We took the toboggan and Simon took his plastic tube ring.

The neighborhood houses were dressed up in snow, with white eyebrows over their windows and beards overhanging their foundation plantings. Other people had built snowfolk. One father was out there with his kids making a dinosaur that had to be seven feet long. It reminded me of a dinosaur my dad had built for me once on the beach. He'd been fun on the beach that week of summer vacation, but we hadn't gone again. One of these days I should write him a letter and remind him about that vacation. Usually I just write to thank him for birthday or Christmas presents—when he remembers to send any. But he'd probably like to get a letter from me just because, and Youn Hee was right—I could try some to please him. After all, he is my father, and you only get one natural one.

As I expected, the snow on the golf course hill was packed down nicely and criss-crossed with ski and toboggan tracks. The grove of evergreens at the top looked gorgeous trimmed in white. Audrey and Bud were there. Bud had a snowboard, and he let me try it while he took Simon down on my toboggan. Youn Hee said she didn't want to go, that she'd just watch. I figured she'd get pretty cold watching and be ready to try sliding soon enough, so I took Simon down on the toboggan and tumbled him into the snow. We came up laughing, and Youn Hee still didn't budge. Simon showed her how he could go down the less-steep side slope on his plastic tube. She pulled it up to the top for him and he went down again, but she didn't want to try it herself even though she was small enough. Meanwhile Audrey and Bud and I piled three deep on the toboggan and sailed farther out into the field below than anybody had, yelling our heads off all the way. What a ride!

"Come on, Youn Hee," Bud said. "Try it; you'll like it."

"I'll take you down, Youn Hee," Audrey said. "You don't have to go with your wild-woman sister."

"Me wild?" I said. "Look who's talking." I pulled Audrey's scarf up over her nose and she pulled my wool cap down over my eyes.

"Don't fight!" Youn Hee begged us.

"They're just fooling around, Youn Hee," Bud said. "Come on, I'll take you down. You can trust me."

I guess she was tired of shaking her head no, because she said, "Caitlin can take me."

Everybody cheered. I sat behind her and put my arms around her and steered us crosswise down the hill, avoiding the mogul, which was a pretty hefty bump. It was a slow and easy ride. "Did you like it?" I asked eagerly.

"Yes," she said with a smile to prove she meant it.

"Let's go again."

"No," she said. "I go home now."

"Simon won't want to leave yet," I warned her.

"He can stay."

"You mean you trust me? You don't think I'm going to set a bad example and get him in trouble?"

"Caitlin," Youn Hee scolded, "why you make fun of me?"

"I guess because I don't think I am a bad example."

"Sometimes you are."

"Sometimes," I admitted while Youn Hee located her house key in a zippered pocket.

She looked so small and determined as she trudged through the snow on her way home. I wondered if anything I could do would change her mind about me. I even decided to start showing more respect to my elders and see if that would make her like me better. I mean, I was desperate enough to try anything.

Chapter Fifteen

The next day we had to go to school. The snow was still a couple of feet deep, but the roads had been cleared and the school buses were running. Now don't get me wrong. I like school OK. Maybe I don't take it as seriously as Youn Hee does, but I like lunch and gym, and science class—when we get to do group projects. Once I even liked social studies. That was when we built an Indian village in fourth grade. Also, I was looking forward to the medieval festival sixth-graders had in the spring. But if you give me a choice of being indoors or out, I'd just rather be out, especially in the snow, especially in winter.

Anyway, lunchtime came, and Bud and I were doing a snow sculpture outside the cafeteria that we hoped would look like the teacher who always yelled at everybody

when she had hall duty. We did her big
bosoms and duck feet and were getting her
stick arms to look like she was shaking a
finger at somebody when Denise tapped me
on the shoulder.

"Caitlin, you better come see what's going
on in the kindergarten playground."

What was going on was Youn Hee was
yanking on the long hair of a girl twice her
size who was screaming bloody murder and
whaling away at Youn Hee while the kinder-
gartners stood in a circle and watched. I was
sure Youn Hee's chicken bones would crack
any minute if I didn't stop that hulk of a kid
fast.

Just as I was about to jump her, a teacher
arrived. "What's going on here?" she demanded.

Youn Hee looked up at her wide-eyed and
silent. The big girl said, "This kid attacked
me. She just—"

"Hey, wait a minute," I said. "You must
have been doing something bad. Youn Hee
wouldn't beat you up for nothing."

"Well, we'll just let the principal get to
the bottom of this," the teacher said.

Youn Hee gave a fearful glance over her

shoulder at me as the teacher hauled her and the female Godzilla off to the principal's office.

"Simon, what was that all about?" I asked.

"She hit me." He showed me his face.

I gasped when I saw his cut lip and swollen cheek. "We better get you to the nurse. Someone tell his teacher his sister took him to the nurse's office." I pointed at a likely-looking boy. "You, tell his teacher for me. OK?" Then I grabbed Simon's hand and ran.

Our nurse is young and bouncy and cheerful. She checked Simon's teeth. "Nothing loose that I can see," she said. Next she put a cold pack on his cheek and asked him, "So how'd the other fellow make out, Simon?"

"It wasn't a fellow. It was a sister. She hit me."

"Youn Hee hit you?" I asked in disbelief.

"No!" he said. "She hit Bailey's sister because she hit me."

"Oh," I said. "So what did you do to Bailey that made his sister so mad at you?"

"Bull's eye, Detective Caitlin!" the nurse teased.

She might think the whole thing was funny, but I had the feeling we were in big trouble—at least Youn Hee and Simon were.

"I didn't do *nothing* to Bailey," Simon protested loudly as he held the cold pack to his cheek. "Bailey's my friend."

"Bailey's the little redheaded kid?" I asked to get the cast of characters straight in my mind.

"Right. Bailey."

"So then what did you do to his sister that made her so mad?"

"Just because Bailey's sled broke."

"You broke it?"

"It broke. He let me use it."

"What did you do with it that it broke?" I asked.

"Nothing." His shrug had a guilty lift to it.

"Simon!"

"Well, there's no hills, so I sledded it down the big slide and it broke."

"I see," I said. "So then what?"

"So then Bailey cried and his sister came to take him home, and she yelled at me because the sled broke."

"Bailey's sister yelled at you."

"Yes, and she said, 'Pay for it,' and I said, 'I got no money,' and she said, 'Well, then your mother's gonna pay,' and I said, 'No.' So then she hit me."

"Wow! And Youn Hee saw her hit you?"

"I don't know. All of a sudden somebody jumped on Bailey's sister's back, and it was Youn Hee." His eyes widened as he remembered. "And she hit her and pulled her hair, and Youn Hee was winning the fight." He looked at me in wonder. I thought it was pretty wonderful, too. Youn Hee had guts, at least when her family was in danger she did.

I wondered how she was doing with Mr. Pollock. The last time we'd been in his office had been when Simon was on trial for swinging those chukka sticks around. Youn Hee had been too scared to open her mouth then. She was probably even more scared right now, scared enough to forget the English words for what she wanted to say. She needed help. But my help? Rats! Youn Hee was right about respect. If I'd showed some before, Mr. Pollock would be more likely to listen to me now. On the other hand, who else knew that Youn Hee had just come to her little brother's defense?

I thanked the nurse and hustled Simon off to the principal's office. Nobody was in the secretary's pen. She was probably out to lunch. I could hear Mr. Pollock's voice pounding away behind his closed office door. Taking a deep breath, I revved up my courage and knocked.

"Yes?" He growled.

"It's me, Caitlin," I said. "Can I come in, Mr. Pollock?"

I took his grunt as permission and opened the door. Sure enough, Youn Hee was drooping in front of his desk, while Bailey's sister stood there boldly, like she'd just won the first round.

"It wasn't Youn Hee's fault," I blurted out. "She was just trying to keep Bailey's sister from beating Simon up."

Mr. Pollock folded his hands in his lap and leaned back in his chair. The smudges under his eyes weren't promising. "Youn Hee admits she attacked first," he said.

"Only to protect Simon. Look." I pulled Simon out from behind me to show off his banged-up face. "I had to take him to the nurse's office."

"He broke my brother's sled," Bailey's sister bellowed. "That Simon's always taking things from my brother. He's a regular hood. Him and his sister ought to go back to Korea where they belong."

"Hey," I jumped in. "That's not fair. Simon doesn't steal things. Bailey's his friend. They share their toys sometimes, but Simon's a good kid and he wouldn't take anything that wasn't his. And we'll pay for the sled, don't worry." I could have killed Bailey's sister for saying that about Korea. Now Youn Hee would be convinced everybody here was prejudiced.

"And I'm to take your word for this, Caitlin?" Mr. Pollock asked me.

We were back to the sugar in the gas tank incident again. "I always tell the truth, Mr. Pollock. Ask Bailey if you don't believe me."

"The point here is that settling things by hitting people is wrong," Mr. Pollock said. "And while you may be truthful, you're also a slugger, or do you deny that?"

"I've changed, Mr. Pollock," I said. Well, I was going to. He frowned at me. I hoped he wasn't remembering the time I'd been called into his office for evening up things at the basketball game when the gym teacher hadn't seen Audrey being tripped.

"All right then, let me do some thinking here," Mr. Pollock said. He covered his mouth with his long fingers and his hooded eyes studied us all darkly. It took a while before the gavel fell.

"What I want," he said finally, "is written reports from all of you on what you think happened and how it should be settled fairly. Bring them to me tomorrow morning before school begins, and we'll deal with this then. You can return to your classes."

"I'm supposed to take my brother to the dentist," Bailey's sister said. "We're late already."

"Well, hurry up then," Mr. Pollock said. He waved Bailey's sister out of his office.

I was about to follow Youn Hee and Simon out when Mr. Pollock said quietly, "Caitlin."

"Yes?" I hesitated with one foot out the door.

"I do believe you tell the truth."

"You do?" I smiled with relief. That

169

meant I could go on to high school someday without trailing a bad reputation behind me. "Good," I said. "Bye, Mr. Pollock."

Youn Hee crept through the rest of the day as if she wanted to hide in her own skin. Even on the way home she barely said a word or raised her eyes. I wondered what was wrong with her. She could at least have thanked me for sticking up for her. If I'd left her on her own, Bailey's sister *would* have been the winner.

Writing the report was a cinch that night. I just told what had happened, and Youn Hee and Simon signed it. Mom added a note saying she'd pay for the sled and that she would deduct some of the cost from Simon's allowances.

Youn Hee's report was very short. She said, "I am very sorry for fighting. I promise not to do again."

When she finished it, she went up to our room to read, and Simon and I watched TV for a while. By the time I got to bed, Youn Hee's light was out, and she was just a lump under the covers.

" 'Night, Youn Hee," I said as I slid into my bed. I was kind of wishing we could talk about what had happened, but I couldn't tell if she was still awake. I listened. When I heard some sniffling, I turned on the reading light over my bed. "What's wrong?"

Youn Hee was crying all right. She had her head under the pillow and I could see her shoulders heaving. "Hey," I said. "Come out from under there and tell me what you're crying about, Youn Hee. Please."

"I got in trouble," she said, "and now Mr. Pollock will send me back to the orphanage."

"What? No, he won't, Youn Hee." I shook my head. "You've got it all wrong. You were a hero. You *were,* Youn Hee. The way you defended Simon was really brave."

"But Mr. Pollock said no hitting."

"Right, but Bailey's sister hit Simon first, and she's bigger than Simon. She's the one who was bad, not you."

Youn Hee clutched the pillow to her chest. "You sure?"

"Positive. . . . Youn Hee? I thought you wanted to go back to the orphanage."

She looked shocked and she said, "Oh no, Caitlin, I like it better here."

"Really?" I started a smile that grew so wide it felt like it was rising off the sides of my face. Youn Hee would never know how happy she'd just made me. Imagine, despite everything in Korea being better—and despite the fact that I was a bad example to her brother—she wanted to stay here!

Chapter Sixteen

At the beginning of February a letter finally came from Hee Sook. The envelope with the Korean return address was there when we got home from school. Youn Hee clapped her hands when she saw it. "Hee Sook wrote me a letter," she said as if it were a surprise and not something we'd been waiting for for weeks and weeks.

I expected Youn Hee might want to hole up in private somewhere to read her letter, but she sat right down at the kitchen table and opened it while Simon and I were having our cookies and hot chocolate. The smile never left Youn Hee's face as she read to herself.

"Want to hear what it says?" she asked us when she'd finished.

"Of course we do," I said.

"I don't know Hee Sook, do I?" Simon asked.

"We all know Hee Sook even if we haven't met her," I said.

"Hee Sook is my dearest friend," Youn Hee told him.

That shook me. I guess I had hopes of being her dearest friend since she didn't want me as her sister, but now it seemed not being Korean kept me out of the running for best friend, too.

Youn Hee rattled the paper and began translating slowly. "Hee Sook says: 'Thank you so much for the very beautiful nice presents. I liked them all. And I thank you so much. Every night I think about you, Youn Hee, and I am glad you are lucky in America, but I miss you. Every night I miss you, and I pray for you.

" 'I wish you would come back and visit me someday. When I grow up and earn money, I will save and send you a ticket. Maybe you can bring your whole family and show them Korea. I am so glad you have a nice new family and your brother is together with you now, but don't forget me.

" 'Your friend, Hee Sook.' "

Youn Hee had tears in her eyes when she looked up.

"She sounds really nice," I said.

"She is."

"Are you going to write to her?"

"Tonight."

"Well, tell her I said hi, and that I'd like to be her friend, too, and maybe she can come to America and visit us someday."

"Yes." Youn Hee nodded.

I tried not to be jealous of Hee Sook. I reminded myself she was in Korea and I was here with Youn Hee. Besides, Hee Sook was an orphan, and I had Mom. I even had Dad a little. He'd called when he got the letter I'd written him, and he'd sounded pleased and talked about getting together in the spring. He'd been kind of vague about it, but at least it was a possibility—one Youn Hee and Hee Sook would never have. Reminding myself that I was lucky helped some, but I still had a few jealous lumps, like zits that wouldn't go away.

The first Saturday in February we spent what seemed like an ordinary day indoors because it was sleeting and nasty outside. Afterward Mom pointed out that the day had been an example of how different things were now between Youn Hee and Simon and me.

At breakfast I asked Youn Hee, "So what are you going to do all day? Read?"

"Play," Simon said.

We agreed to play Make a Face with him, but when we'd eaten the waffles Mom made us, Simon decided he wanted to watch cartoons on TV for a while. "Then we play," he promised us as if we might be disappointed.

"We could start our social studies project," Youn Hee suggested.

"But it's not due for more than a month," I protested.

"If we start now, we'll make a better castle," Youn Hee said. We'd signed up to build a castle together as our project for the medieval festival.

I agreed grudgingly, but once we started drawing up plans of what we were going to build, I got excited and enjoyed myself. In fact, when Simon came to our room where Youn Hee and I were working on our big desk, I didn't want to stop.

"We're busy now, Simon. You play by yourself for a while, and we'll do something with you later."

"Now," he said.

"After lunch," I said.

He promptly went over to Youn Hee and leaned against her arm and coaxed, "Play with me?"

She was concentrating on drawing a design for a torture chamber. "Don't shake my arm, Simon," she said.

"I don't have anyone to play with," he whined.

"Simon"—Youn Hee's pretty face frowned at him sternly—"you must learn to play by yourself. Now go find something to do." She turned back to her drawing.

Simon sniffed and trotted downstairs where I heard him complaining to Mom, "It's no fair. Why can't I have a brother? Two sisters is no fair."

"They play with you a lot, Simon," Mom said.

"No they don't. They talk all the time together and don't let me listen. And they don't let me in the bathroom and they lock me out. And they always tell me what to do. I need a brother."

"How about a hamster or a turtle?" Mom suggested.

I listened, giggling, and looked at Youn

Hee, who had also been listening. Her eyes were laughing with me. After lunch we did play with Simon for a couple of hours. Then when the roads were salted, Mom took us all to the mall and Simon got the most adorable guinea pig, fluffy and white with a pink nose. He had to keep it in his room away from me because I started to sneeze the minute I held it, but Youn Hee and Simon could play with it, and they let me name it Snooze.

"Snooze?" Simon questioned me.

"Yeah. It sounds funny, doesn't it?"

"Yeah," he agreed. So Snooze it was.

Anyway, what Mom said about that day was it showed that Youn Hee and I were sharing Simon instead of fighting each other for him, and I guess that's true. Sometimes Youn Hee and I both love him and sometimes we hate him. Sometimes he does things with just one of us, sometimes with both, but we also do things all together, which is how it's supposed to be, I think.

My birthday comes right in the middle of the vacation week we get around President's Day, when everybody here goes skiing or to sunny Florida. That year my best friends were all unavailable. Audrey was at a ski lodge with her family. Bud was visiting his mother's other husband—not his father but his mother's second husband, who was only his stepfather but Bud and he love each other. Denise was in bed with the flu. I moaned and groaned so much about what a terrible birthday it was going to be that Mom got kind of touchy about it.

"Don't you think you can have fun with your own family?" she asked me.

"Yeah, sure," I said, "but a birthday should be a special celebration, not just what you do every day."

"It will be special," Mom said. "I'll think of something."

Well, she did. I'm an Aquarian, so what we did for my birthday was stay overnight at a motel with a big indoor swimming pool surrounded by tropical plants and colored lights. It was like being on a tropical island. Simon went wild over the game room and wanted to spend all his time playing the video games. While he raced down electronic mountain roads and fought battles with alien monsters, Youn Hee and I played Ping-Pong. Even though she's grown a lot,

I'm still twice her size, so I have a longer reach, but she'd learned how to play in Korea—and Ping-Pong was her sport all right. She beat me.

"I'm sorry!" she said as if it were a tragedy.

"What for?" I said. "I'm glad you won."

"But it's your birthday."

"Right, and I love a challenge. Come on, let's play again." It took me four games before I beat her one.

We spent hours in the pool. Youn Hee doesn't know how to swim, so I pulled her and Simon around in the shallow end until I got tired. Then we took turns jumping in at the shallow end and ducking underwater to pick up a quarter that Mom tossed for us.

At dinner the waiter asked who the birthday girl was, and Youn Hee said, "My sister, Caitlin." I must have sat there with my jaw hanging for a minute or more. It was the first time Youn Hee had ever actually called me *sister*. I got great presents: my own tape deck and a suitcase and new clothes, a chocolate Valentine heart from Simon, and a tiny stuffed unicorn from Youn Hee. Oh, and Dad sent me money in a really nice "Daughter" card. But Youn Hee's calling me sister—that was my best present.

I told Mom she'd given me the most terrific birthday I'd ever had, and it really was. On top of that, when I got back to school my friends had a belated birthday party for me, so I had a double-header celebration.

That spring, when the six months' probation period was past and we were officially a three-kid family, Denise told me something weird.

"You know," she said while we were washing our hands in the girls' room at school, "Youn Hee's getting to look like you."

"Oh, come on," I said. "She's grown a lot, but I'm still much bigger. And my hair's light brown and curly, and hers is black and straight, and—"

Denise was shaking her head, and I could see she was serious. "Well, what do you mean, she looks like me?" I demanded.

"I guess it's how you walk, kind of chin up and prancy. Youn Hee walks the same way. And the way you wrinkle up one side of your face when you don't like something?

She does that. And, I don't know. . . . She just looks like you."

I grinned. "Well, why shouldn't she? We're sisters, you know," I said.

That night after we'd turned out the lights and were ready to go to sleep, Youn Hee said to me, "You're being good now, Caitlin. I never thought you would behave good in school, but you do now. Better, anyway."

I smiled, remembering how polite I'd been to the lunch aide who accused me of popping paper bags when it hadn't been me at all.

"Well," I said to Youn Hee, "I never thought you'd get to be American, but you did—and fast, too."

"I'm *not* American. I'm Korean. . . . And maybe a little bit American, but not much."

"OK," I teased. "So since you're my sister, I must be a little bit Korean."

"No, Caitlin," Youn Hee informed me. "We can be different and still belong together. In America everybody is different and still belongs."

"Yes," I said, and grinned to myself. She had gotten the message so well she thought it was her own idea. But I was the one who'd thought it first, *said* it first in November when she came. We are different, like most people in a family are different, but our hearts are bound up together. We belong to each other, Youn Hee and Simon and Mom and me. We're a family. You can just look at us and tell.